Cont...

1	Well Met	1
2	Love in the Air	12
3	Parting	23
4	Commitment	34
5	Tragedy	44
6	Adjustment	55
7	Heart-break	64
8	The Concert	77
9	Salvation	87
10	Wedding Bells	96

Well Met

Thembi looked anxiously at her watch. It would be a miracle if she caught the bus. Saturday morning in Eloff Street was pretty hectic, and she had just reached the crossing when she saw her bus pull in. As she stepped down from the pavement she realised that the traffic light was amber. She hesitated for a fraction of a second before deciding to risk it.

There was a sudden squeal of brakes and she sensed rather than saw a large car stop within inches of her. She heard the dull thud of a door banging and felt her arm roughly taken in a strong grip.

'What the hell do you think you're doing, *sisi*?' demanded a furious voice. 'Couldn't you see the light was against you?'

Thembi trembled violently as she gazed mutely into the brown, glittering eyes set in a ruggedly masculine brown face. His expression softened fractionally as he spoke with exasperation, raking one hand through black, salon-styled hair.

'Are you all right? I didn't hurt you, did I?'

Thembi shook her head. 'I'm sorry. I was in a hurry to catch a bus and thought I could make it,' she said with as much dignity as she could muster, though her voice shook.

'Well, you shouldn't take such chances. You may not be so lucky next time. Do you realise just how close I came to hitting you?' He was looking at her intently. 'You're very grey. Are you sure you're all right?' he went on, as he wrapped his fingers around her upper arm.

At his touch she felt as if a charge of electricity had shot through her. Instinctively she pulled away from him.

'I'm OK,' she replied. 'Really I am.'

'Then please get back on the pavement and wait for the

green light.' His parting shot was almost drowned by the noise of impatient motorists honking their horns and shouting to know what the hold-up was.

Thembi watched as the man walked quickly back to his car, got in and drove away.

A titter ran through the rather large group of people that had gathered and she felt herself flush. Her bus, of course, had long since gone. Straightening her spine and lifting her head proudly, she turned away and went into a nearby Wimpy Bar for a Coke. She sat quietly until she felt calmer.

Presently, deciding to put the whole incident behind her, she paid her bill and walked out into the bright sunshine.

———————— ♥ ————————

There can't be many places as lovely or peaceful as an autumn twilight in the Transvaal, thought Thembi two weeks later as she stood on the veranda of her home in Roseacres, a new suburb on the West Rand. She breathed in the scent of roses from the well-tended garden. There wasn't much traffic this early on a Saturday evening, and she savoured the peace, knowing that soon the endless stream of cars and motor bikes going into Hillbrow for a Saturday night boogie would shatter the tranquillity.

Although the sun had already sunk below the horizon there were one or two distant clouds, delicately tinged with pink, reflecting the last rays of the sun which was already losing its intense summer heat. Not a breath of wind disturbed the lacy traces of white scattered overhead.

Everything was ready for her guests. Thembi's mother was giving a party for her twenty-fourth birthday. Thembi had thrown herself into the preparations with enthusiasm, helping mainly with the cooking.

With a deep sigh of contentment she turned, ready to go indoors. Her Grecian style white gown, shot through with silver thread, outlined her high, firm breasts and emphasised

2

her waist, slender hips and long, tapering legs. With one shoulder bare, the garment draped to the waist, then cunningly draped again to the hem, with a split up one side, an ideal foil for her smooth, creamy, ebony skin.

Around her neck was a string of matched pearls, her birthday gift from her parents. A single pearl glimmered in each earlobe.

She looked down at the thin silver straps of her evening sandals and smiled with pleasure. Shoes were her greatest weakness. The previous evening her feet had been in ice-skating boots. She loved skating and, together with her cousin, Nomalizo, went to the Carlton Skyrink as often as possible. Nomalizo was a nursing sister and was often on night duty. When she was working, Thembi went skating with a crowd of high-spirited young people that the girls had become friendly with.

Thembi walked into the lounge and looked around. She was filled with gratitude and a deep sense of well-being. She and her parents had strung streamers across the room and clusters of balloons made the room look festive. The large, comfortable sofa and chairs had been pushed back against the wall to make room for dancing. Thembi's music centre, with a stack of records and tapes, was set back from the dancing area.

The pastel walls provided a muted background for the rich dark green tapestry on the furniture and the heavy gold velvet floor to ceiling curtains. The champagne colour of the carpet was flecked with brown and green.

A large picture of a stormy sea hung on one wall. Two smaller pictures of the peaceful countryside on the other walls provided an interesting and calming contrast. The room was brightly lit by two reading lamps and a track of three spotlights.

Standing in the middle of the room, looking around him, was Thembi's father. He turned and walked towards her, taking both her hands in his. He shook his head, a look of bemusement on his face.

'You look beautiful, Thembi. You could be a model on the cover of *Drum* magazine! I can't believe this elegant young lady is the same little schoolgirl in a gymslip who used to always be in trouble. I'm very proud of you,' he said, kissing her cheek.

'Thank you, Baba,' she answered with a shimmer of tears enhancing the brilliance of her eyes.

Maliyeza Gumbi was a tall, healthy man of fifty. He worked out at the local Health and Racquet Club twice a week, and now held a high-ranking position in a retail store in Sandton City. The harsh days of poverty in the ghetto of Soweto were indelibly imprinted on all their minds. It had been a long, tough haul for Maliyeza, trying to complete his matric by correspondence at night, while working during the day to support his family, who were very proud of him. There was a deep bond of mutual love and respect between them all.

'So there you two are!' exclaimed Thembi's mother as she came into the room. 'Thembi, that dress is the most beautiful I have ever seen you in. You look lovely. But don't you think that slit is a bit daring?'

'Not a bit,' laughed Maliyeza. 'This is the look of the new generation. It's very sexy.'

'Oh, do you think I am showing too much leg, Mama?' asked Thembi with a worried frown.

'No. I am only teasing,' replied her mother, her eyes twinkling merrily. She was a well-groomed woman and had a lively sense of humour and depth of compassion which was easily aroused, especially where children were concerned.

The first guests to arrive were Nomalizo and her mother.

'Naledi!' said Thembi's mother, hugging her twin sister and kissing her cheek. 'Hello, Nomalizo. I am so glad that you are off-duty tonight. Where is your father?'

'He had to work late,' replied Nomalizo with a smile. 'He

4

was doing stock-taking today and hopes to get here before the party is over, but he didn't seem too optimistic when he left home. You know what taking stock is like. Anyway, happy birthday, Thembi,' she said, handing a silver wrapped parcel to her cousin. 'You look beautiful. Where did you get that dress?'

'I'll take you there next time you want something special,' Thembi promised.

'Thanks. You know, that hairstyle really is something,' replied Nomaiizo. The cousins linked arms and walked through to the dining room, chattering away with easy familiarity as they went.

As they were both only children and the families had lived close together in Soweto, the girls had gone to school together and grown up more like sisters than cousins.

'Thank God there were no last-minute emergencies this afternoon, and I was able to get away from the hospital on time,' sighed Nomalizo. 'I haven't been to a party in months and I've been looking forward to this one all week. The lounge looks lovely and I can just feel that we're going to have a super time tonight. Oh boy, oh boy!' she exclaimed as they entered the dining room, admiring the buffet table which had been set in the centre of the room, allowing free access to the mouth-watering fare that had been laid out. 'Your mother has really excelled herself this time.'

'My mother and her apprentice, if you don't mind,' laughed Thembi.

'Oh? I beg your pardon, Miss Apprentice,' laughed her cousin in reply. 'And I suppose your mother still found time to go to the home as usual?'

'Of course. I doubt if anything short of an earthquake would keep her away from those kids,' replied Thembi affectionately.

Dikeledi Gumbi spent as many hours as she could in her off-time at a home of safety for physically, mentally and emotionally abused township children. She would sit for hours reading to them, telling them folktales or playing games with them. She was a social worker, and her job often took her to the home, where she voluntarily put in far more hours than she needed to. The children all adored her.

The two young women surveyed the laden table. Canapés were set out in rows on gleaming glass plates. Cocktail onions and other extravagant titbits had been lavishly used to garnish the biscuits with piped fillings of different flavoured creamed eggs and cheeses. Stuffed baby tomatoes and onions added colour to the attractive display. Plates of sandwiches and bowls of nuts and potato crisps filled every available spot on the table.

On a modest sideboard against one wall was a stand set over candle flames holding a bowl of curry and one of rice, with plates, cutlery and paper napkins nearby. Next to the curry was an enticingly laid-out platter of cold meats and chicken, and cream-topped trifles and a fresh fruit salad were there for anyone looking for something sweet. Later in the evening small sausage rolls and tiny meat pies would be served.

'I'm starving,' said Nomalizo. 'I missed lunch today. We were busy with an emergency case and I didn't notice the time.' She popped a sandwich into her mouth.

Nomalizo was a very pretty, slender young woman with stylish close-cropped hair and sparkling eyes set in a serene face. She was very compassionate and ideally suited to being a nurse. The close-fitting dress of midnight blue taffeta accentuated her trim figure.

'How are things at your office?' she asked Thembi.

'Fine,' was the happy reply. Thembi enjoyed her nine-to-five job as a senior secretary to one of the editors of a large daily Johannesburg newspaper.

The other guests began arriving, and soon the house was ringing with the sound of laughter, chatter and music.

Thembi was standing with a group of friends when she felt her arm being taken in a gentle hold. Turning her head, she found Roy, one of her skating friends, standing beside her.

'Happy birthday, Thembi,' he said, kissing her on the cheek and handing her a gaily wrapped gift.

'Thanks, Roy,' she smiled. 'I haven't seen you for quite a while!'

'I've been studying for an exam and haven't seen anyone for quite a while,' he replied, his blue eyes sparkling as he ran his hands through the mop of golden blond curls which he had difficulty in keeping slicked down. Roy was twenty-seven years old, a tall, good-looking man. He and Thembi had gone out a few times since they had met six months earlier, and were very much at ease in each other's company. 'Would you like to have dinner with me tomorrow night to celebrate my last exam for the time being?' he asked.

'Thanks, Roy. I'd like that.'

'I'll pick you up at seven. Ah, there's Nomalizo. I must go and say hello. I haven't seen her in ages either.' With that he turned and walked towards Thembi's cousin.

Thembi heard her father call her name behind her and she was smiling as she turned around.

For a moment she felt quite dizzy, as if the floor had tilted beneath her feet. The smile faded from her lips as she found herself gazing into the glittering eyes of the man standing next to her father – the man who had so nearly knocked her down two weeks earlier!

For a moment the room and everything else faded into the background and she was aware of nothing but him as their eyes met and locked. It was as if the world held only the two of them.

He looked equally stunned. Suddenly he smiled, and his eyes lit up.

Thembi snapped out of her trance-like state as she saw her father propel his companion towards her.

'Thembi, I'd like you to meet Mduduzi Mkhize. We've met a number of times and again at the meeting I went to last week. He is an Industrial Relations consultant and it is men like him that we call on to help with staff disputes and problems,' said Maliyeza. 'Mduduzi, this is my daughter, Thembi. It's *her* birthday.'

'Happy birthday, Thembi,' said Mduduzi, handing her a gift. He took her hand and held it in his firm, warm clasp. 'I'm delighted to meet you. When your father said that I should come around to his daughter's birthday party tonight I had no idea it would be such a large affair.' His eyes twinkled with devilment as he blatantly continued to hold her hand, studying her heavily fringed eyes and small nose above well-defined, slightly sensuous lips.

Still feeling slightly unnerved, she pulled her hand away and gave him a shy smile. 'You are most welcome and I hope you enjoy the evening with us.' As she was speaking she was wondering if he would say anything about their previous encounter. She hoped not. She didn't want her parents to know about it.

'Thank you. I'm sure I will,' he smiled.

Maliyeza turned to Mduduzi. 'Excuse us, Thembi,' he said. 'Come along, Mduduzi, we'll get a drink and then I'll introduce you to my wife.'

As they walked away, Thembi turned back to her friends, but she was aware of Mduduzi Mkhize's presence, even though she could not see him. It wasn't long before she felt the hairs prickling at the nape of her neck and she knew instinctively that he was standing behind her.

Slowly she turned to face him.

By silent, mutual consent, they moved away, and when they were apart from the crowd, she turned her head and looked at him. He was regarding her intently. His expression was serious.

'Don't worry, I won't say anything about the other day,'

8

he said. 'Somehow I don't think you told your parents, did you?'

'No, I didn't. How did you know?'

'You have very beautiful but extremely expressive eyes, and at the moment they are very apprehensive,' he replied softly. 'Thembi, I meant what I said then. You shouldn't take such chances with the traffic. You know that people drive like cowboys on the roads these days. I still go cold when I think of how close I came to knocking you down.'

Gazing at him she saw a man over six feet tall in a superbly cut grey suit which fitted perfectly, clearly showing that there was no surplus flesh on his powerful body. Thembi judged him to be in his early thirties. She could feel strength and latent power flowing from him as he towered above her. She saw again the fashionable haircut which accentuated his broad, intellectual forehead. At the corners of his eyes were tiny laughter lines, and Thembi was amazed at how clearly she remembered the details of his features, considering the circumstances of their last, brief meeting.

'Thank you, Mr Mkhize, for keeping quiet about it,' she said in tones so low they were almost inaudible. 'You are right and I promise I'll never be so foolish again. I got the fright of my life and I learnt a lesson I'll never forget.'

'Good. And it's Mduduzi, Thembi, never Mr Mkhize, please. Not to you. I want to speak to you but it's rather crowded and noisy in here. Could we go outside for a while?' he changed the subject briskly, easing away the embarrassment she had been feeling. Thembi nodded her head. Taking her glass from her fingers and placing it with his on a nearby table, he cupped her elbow and led her out on to the veranda.

The air was cool, the sky clear and star-studded. A full moon hung overhead and its silver light threw the surrounding trees and shrubs into brilliant relief. Thembi breathed a sigh of deep contentment.

The noise of the music and laughter inside mingled with that of the traffic from the street. Mduduzi turned to her.

'I can't believe I'm here and that I've met you again. You won't believe how many times during the past two weeks your image has haunted me,' he said with quiet intensity. 'Some of them have been at damned awkward times, believe me. In the middle of a discussion which needed absolute concentration I'd suddenly see your huge frightened eyes and that would be that.' He gave a short, self-deprecating laugh as he scratched the back of his head. 'Nothing like that has ever happened to me before. Then tonight you turned around when your father spoke and I felt as if I had been pole-axed. For a moment there I thought I was hallucinating. I could see nothing but you.'

'I, too, couldn't believe it when I saw you,' she whispered in reply.

He took one of her hands in both of his and lifted it to his mouth, kissing each finger before turning it over and then planting a kiss on the palm. He then gently closed her fingers around it.

'Have dinner with me tomorrow night?' he asked, still holding her hand and looking deep into her eyes. Thembi felt her heart thudding against her ribs, every nerve-end tingling vibrantly with supercharged sensitivity. She felt overwhelmed by the sheer animal magnetism which emanated from him and found herself trembling.

She shook her head. 'I'm sorry, Mduduzi, I already have a date,' she replied with genuine regret in her voice.

'Break it,' he said, squeezing her hand tightly, hurting her fingers.

'No,' she said, pulling her hand away. 'I wouldn't do that to you if it was the other way round, and I won't do it to Roy. I'm sorry.'

'He means something special to you, this Roy?' he asked

10

with a suggestion of irritation in his voice and a frown creasing his forehead.

'He's just a very good friend,' she smiled.

He relaxed and released his breath. 'Forgive me. I had no right to ask you that,' he said ruefully. 'But having found you so suddenly and unexpectedly, I'd very much like to spend some time with you, get to know you. It's as simple as that. Monday night then?' He cocked his head to one side, waiting for her answer.

'Yes, thank you. I'd like that very much.'

He smiled at her. 'Come now, we must go back inside. I've monopolised you enough for one evening. After all, it is your party, isn't it? In any case, I want to dance with you. Nice and slowly. It'll give me a good excuse to hold you in my arms,' he teased.

She laughed softly as he led her back into the house.

2

Love in the Air

The first people they saw were Nomalizo and Roy, who were standing together and talking.

'Mduduzi, I'd like you to meet my cousin Nomalizo and my friend Roy,' said Thembi, turning to smile at him. 'Nomalizo, Roy, this is Mduduzi Mkhize, a friend of my father.'

Roy and Mduduzi shook hands, and Nomalizo smiled at him.

'Hi! It's nice to meet you,' she said then turned to Thembi. 'OK for Thursday night?' she asked.

'For sure,' replied Thembi with a grin. 'Nothing would keep me away from the rink – and you know it.'

Mduduzi raised his eyebrows quizzically. 'Ice skating?' he asked. Thembi nodded her head. 'Is it a private party or can anyone join in?' he asked with a smile.

Thembi looked at him blankly for a moment. 'You mean you want to go with us?'

'If I may,' he replied. 'Unless you think I'm too old, of course?' This was said with a teasing smile of pure devilment. Thembi flushed with embarrassment, but joined in the general laughter. 'What about you, Roy? Are you going as well?' Roy promptly agreed.

'Are you any good at it?' Mduduzi asked, looking at Thembi.

'Good at it?' interrupted Nomalizo laughingly. 'Thembi was in the chorus of the last Ice Capades. The show was a huge success.'

'Are you serious?' asked Mduduzi, obviously impressed. 'I saw that show. It was spectacular.'

'Yes,' replied Nomalizo. 'You're going to have your time

12

cut out trying to keep up with her. When Thembi's on the ice, she never knows when to stop!'

'I'll just have to try, then, won't I?' Mduduzi said softly. 'Now, if you will excuse us, we are going to dance.' Taking her arm, he led Thembi on to the dance floor. The lights had been dimmed and they joined the other two couples already there. After a moment's hesitation, Thembi relaxed against him, giving herself up to the sheer rapture of dancing with someone whose steps matched hers perfectly. He gathered her close and let his cheek rest lightly on the crown of her head, while hers nestled snugly into the hollow of his shoulder. She could smell the faint musky fragrance of his aftershave mingled with the clean male odour of him.

She gave a small sigh of contentment. This feeling of having been waiting all her life for this moment, the inevitability of their meeting, was madness, she thought.

'You feel it too, don't you, Thembi?' he murmured huskily, pulling away slightly from her in order to put a finger under her chin and lift her face to his.

'Do I?' she teased gently and could feel the warmth of a faint flush sweeping up her neck and into her cheeks, as the expression on her face revealed that she understood and agreed with him.

'Yes. You must know this was meant to be. You must know that tonight was no chance meeting,' he replied earnestly.

They had stopped dancing and were swaying together to the beat of the music, totally absorbed in each other. She gazed at him helplessly then nodded her head and shyly dropped her face from his intense scrutiny. She felt his body tense as his arms tightened around her and hers groped instinctively for the warmth of his neck.

He lowered his head and sought her mouth in a tender, almost reverent kiss which evoked an equally gentle and natural response. He lifted his head and stared down at her

13

with eyes that glittered with simmering passion. She was caught up in an unexpected and totally alien feeling of rapture, and something he saw in her face was his undoing. With a smothered groan he crushed her to him and his mouth took hers with a devastating intimacy which sent her senses reeling, and unaccustomed desire flared through her like a bush fire. She felt his body shudder against hers.

'I've been wanting to do that from the moment I set eyes on you tonight,' he murmured.

Thembi had often been kissed, but nothing had prepared her for the sudden spiralling of her senses and wild exhilaration as she clung desperately to the muscular line of his broad shoulders without realising what she was doing. He was totally, dominantly male and she rejoiced in her frailer femininity. Suddenly realising where they were they released their grip on each other.

'My God, Thembi, I think we had better go and find something cold to drink,' Mduduzi said with a shaky laugh. 'I don't usually behave like this at a first meeting. I think you've cast a spell over me!'

Her answering laughter rang out clearly and with obvious enjoyment. 'I've been called many things in my time, but never before have I been called a witch.'

He grinned, then taking her hand led her through to the dining room. They went to the buffet, helped themselves, then joined her parents and their guests. The rest of the evening was spent either dancing, or by unspoken, mutual consent, mingling together with her guests. They were vibrantly aware of each other, of their need not to be parted, to be no more than hand-touching distance apart.

Towards midnight the party started to break up and Mduduzi was among the last to leave. He said goodnight to Maliyeza and Dikeledi, thanking them for a most enjoyable evening.

'Our pleasure,' said Maliyeza, shaking his hand. 'I'm very

14

glad you came tonight. We'd very much like to have you come again. Keep in touch.'

'Thanks, I'll do that,' he replied and Thembi had to turn her head to prevent herself from laughing as she saw his lips twitch mischievously, despite the serious expression on his face.

He stood back while Thembi said goodnight to everyone else, then she turned to him and they walked outside together.

In the quiet stillness of the night he faced her and of their own accord his arms closed around her, pulling her slowly and unresistingly towards him, moulding her slender frame to his strength. He bent his head and his lips covered hers, seeking, exploring, persuading and finally devouring in a draining, drugging kiss that neither had the wish nor the ability at that moment to end.

They pressed tightly together, eager for the touch and taste of each other, wanting to prolong the pleasure they felt together. They were both trembling and breathing roughly when he finally lifted his head. As he gazed down at her face, passion and desire arced between them. Giving her a final, quick hug he pulled away.

'I'll be here at seven-thirty on Monday,' he said. He placed his hands on her shoulders and looked deep into her eyes. 'Now go inside before you catch a chill. Goodnight, sweet Thembi. Sleep well,' he said, kissing her quickly and lightly on her forehead. He walked away towards his car and she turned and went back into the house.

'You and Mduduzi seemed to get on well together, Thembi,' said Maliyeza, as they were clearing up. His daughter turned her face away, pretending to plump up a cushion before putting it back in its proper place on the sofa.

'He's a very charming man, Baba, and I'm glad he came tonight. Thanks again to both of you for a wonderful evening,' she said, kissing each of them on the cheek. 'Now I'm

15

for bed. Goodnight.' She turned and started to walk out of the room.

Pausing at the door she looked back impishly at them, 'I think I forgot to mention that I'm having dinner with Mduduzi on Monday night, and he's coming skating with us on Thursday,' she said, then turned and walked through the door.

'Well, what do you think of that, MaThembi? And there I was telling him to keep in touch,' she heard her father say as she went into her bedroom and closed the door.

———— ♥ ————

Thembi stood in front of the mirror looking critically at herself. Excitement brought warmth to her cheeks and a brilliant sparkle to her eyes. She wore very little make-up: a touch of eye shadow to emphasise her luminous eyes and a trace of lip gloss were enough.

A pencil slim black skirt was teamed with a shimmering gold figure-hugging long sleeved top which fitted to the base of her throat in front and plunged to a V at the back. Gold hoops in her ears were her only adornment. She dabbed some of her favourite perfume behind each ear and on her wrists, then bent to pick up her evening bag and coat.

Never before had she felt so vitally, tinglingly alive or looked forward to an evening with such eagerness combined with nervous anticipation. Tension coiled within her as she thought of Mduduzi. Had there really been that instant, vibrant attraction between them, an inexplicable, almost spiritual pull as they had looked at each other? Was he really as exciting as she remembered, or had it just been an illusion, created by the glamour of the occasion and the knowledge of a shared secret which had drawn her like a magnet?

As she approached the lounge she heard voices and she recognised Mduduzi's voice. She had not heard him arrive. She took a deep breath and with her heart beating wildly she walked into the room.

Her eyes were drawn immediately and irresistibly to him and she found his riveted on her. He stood up as she entered.

'Hello, Thembi,' was all he said while his eyes ranged possessively and appreciatively over her in one sweep. She stood for a moment under his intense scrutiny then returned his greeting.

As they drove away neither seemed able to break the silence.

Finally Mduduzi spoke, telling her where they were going. His voice was flat. Thembi said she was looking forward to the evening. An uneasy silence settled once more over them and the air was charged with tension.

Thembi was frantically trying to think of something to say when he looked sideways at her. 'Dammit, Thembi, I've looked forward so much to tonight. I've thought of little else for the past two days and now I find myself as tongue-tied as some youngster on his first date!' He stretched out his hand and curled his fingers around hers. 'That's better,' he sighed. 'Now I know I didn't dream you.'

She relaxed and gave a low chuckle. 'If it's any consolation, I feel like that too. I thought tonight would never come.' She squeezed his hand. 'I used to feel like this about Christmas.'

All restraint between them disappeared and soon they turned into a brightly lit driveway flanked by well-tended gardens. None of the original beauty or grandeur of the old building had been lost in its conversion into a restaurant.

Mduduzi's hand cupped her elbow as they opened the door and walked into the reception area. Wood panelled walls, a thick deep-pile carpet and an antique reservations desk blended harmoniously. The lighting was soft, and hanging overhead was a magnificent chandelier, its crystal prisms swinging gently in the slight breeze.

'Oh, this is beautiful,' whispered Thembi, looking around. 'Thank you for bringing me here.' He squeezed her arm and smiled at her.

At their table they found themselves screened from the rest of the room by the plants. The soft lights, gentle music and the low hum of conversation and laughter combined to create an atmosphere of secluded intimacy.

Reaching over the table Mduduzi took her hands in his and looked at her for a few seconds. His voice was low and husky when he spoke.

'Oh God, Thembi, you're beautiful. I've been so afraid that I'd find you different to what I remembered. But you're not. Everything about you is perfect.' He lifted her hand to his lips and kissed her fingers, still looking into her eyes.

She was overcome with emotion and had to swallow a couple of times before she could trust herself to speak.

'No, Mduduzi, I'm not perfect. Far from it. I'm human – and like everyone else I have many failings.' She spoke softly, looking earnestly into his eyes. 'But I, too, wondered if you could really be as special as I thought you were or if it was just wishful thinking,' she said, lips smiling and eyes twinkling.

'You picked the damnedest place to say a thing like that,' he said roughly, but she could see that her words pleased him.

They settled back in their seats and after he had ordered wine they studied their menus, commenting now and then on their likes or otherwise of the various dishes. They were not surprised to find how often their tastes coincided.

'Now then, I want to know everything there is to know about Thembi Gumbi,' said Mduduzi after the waiter had taken their order.

They talked and laughed while they ate their dinner and told each other about their childhood, their hopes for the future, their dreams. They touched lightly on politics and religion and she told him about her work and her love for music as well as skating. This led to a lively discussion on music and then books. She learned that, being an Industrial

Relations consultant with a business of his own, his work sometimes took him to other centres; that he was an only child and was very attached to his parents who lived near Cape Town.

He spoke of his cousin Lindi who, when she was eight years old, had lost her parents in a motor car accident. Lindi, who was five years younger than Mduduzi, had been taken in by his parents and they had grown up together. He had looked after and protected her as if she had been his sister. Lindi was now happily married to a farmer in Venda, with two children of her own. They did not see very much of each other these days, although she kept in close contact with his parents.

They were so totally engrossed in each other that when Thembi got up to go to the powder room after they had finished she was surprised to find that they were the only two left in the dining room. Neither of them had realised how late it was.

When he parked at her front door, Mduduzi turned to her. 'Tonight has been wonderful. All I'd hoped it would be and more. You're a very special person, warm and natural and very easy to talk to, with a delightful sense of humour. I'm utterly fascinated by everything about you.'

'Why, thank you, kind sir,' Thembi replied, trying to cover her embarrassment with a joke. 'I've enjoyed this evening very much. Thank you for taking me out,' she added seriously.

'I have tickets for the gala evening of *The Mikado* at the Civic Centre tomorrow night. Would you like to go?' he asked.

'Oh yes, please,' she breathed eagerly, putting her hand out to touch his.

Taking it in his, he played with her fingers and they sat in contented silence for a while. Releasing her hand he moved his arm to encircle her shoulders, turning her to face him.

19

His other hand came up to trace the shape of her cheeks, her nose, her chin, with a touch as light as thistledown. His thumb brushed tenderly across the fullness of her lower lip and she trembled when his mouth replaced it in a slow and druggingly sensuous movement.

She lifted one arm and slid it around his neck while the other one found its way to his waist and then around his body until she was pressed close to him, exulting in the contact, lost to everything but the passion surging through her, setting her blood on fire.

'I've been wanting to do that all evening,' he whispered raggedly, lifting his head to study her face. Her eager response delighted and spurred him on to greater demands. As they clung together she felt as if she had been caught up in the wildly swirling water of a whirlpool, exhilarated beyond anything she had ever known. She was aware of nothing but him; the feel of him, the taste of him, the smell of him. Her hands restlessly stroked his hair, his neck, the wide span of his shoulders.

He groaned deep in his throat as he drew away from her. A shuddering sigh escaped him as his ardent gaze roamed over her eyes, her cheeks and her lips. He released her reluctantly.

'No more, Thembi. I'm a man, not a boy, and we must stop while I'm still able to. This is neither the time nor the place to let this get out of hand,' he added as he felt her bewildered withdrawal. He walked with her to the door, fitted the key and turned the lock, gave her one last lingering kiss then gently pushed her aside.

'Till tomorrow night,' he said softly and was gone.

They went to the operetta and she loved every moment. Mduduzi held her hand and squeezed it, sharing her enchantment.

The lounge lights were still burning when they arrived home.

'Did you enjoy yourselves?' asked Dikeledi.

'It was super, Mama. Wasn't it, Mduduzi?'

'It certainly was,' he replied warmly.

'Of course, we knew Thembi would be in her element,' said Maliyeza. 'She has been studying piano and singing for about four years now,' he added, aware of Mduduzi's interest. 'She recently joined an oratorio choir and they are busy preparing a presentation of *Messiah*.'

'You really are quite a girl, aren't you?' said Mduduzi softly, his eyes caressing her. 'Will you play and sing for me sometime?'

'If you'd like me to.'

'Would you two like some coffee? Or something stronger, Mduduzi?' asked Dikeledi.

'Coffee will be fine, thanks, but I can't stay long. I have an early appointment in the morning and there's some paper-work which must be done before I go to bed tonight,' he replied.

He did not stay long after they had drunk their coffee and after bidding her parents goodnight, he and Thembi walked out of the room together.

On the veranda they turned to each other and as naturally as a homing pigeon she moved into his waiting arms.

At first their kiss was gentle, tinged with a lingering trace of the enjoyment they had shared earlier in the evening. Then suddenly it became a relentless, all-consuming flame threatening to destroy them.

His hands moved restlessly as the fingers of one hand held her head while the other arm was clamped around her shoulders, his fingers kneading the soft flesh of her upper arm.

'My God, I can't seem to get enough of you,' he groaned. 'I can't keep my hands off you and I can't control myself when I'm with you. I simply don't recognise myself any more,' he said, shaking his head.

'I know. It's the same with me,' she replied. 'I've never reacted to anyone as I do to you. Does that make me seem cheap?'

'No. You're being honest and I wouldn't have you any other way,' he replied, putting his forehead to hers and rubbing her nose with his.

Then he straightened up, keeping his arms about her with his hands loosely clasped behind her back.

'What are we doing tomorrow night?' he asked, arrogantly assuming that they would be together.

'You choose. Tonight and Thursday are mine. Tomorrow night is yours,' she replied then flushed heatedly as she realised what she had said.

He gave a spontaneous shout of delighted laughter. 'Thembi, you're enchanting, you really are. Never mind, I'll not take advantage of that very tempting invitation. I'll surprise you. Don't dress up; jeans and a t-shirt will be fine.'

The following night he refused to tell her where they were going until she realised that they were going to the circus. Neither of them had been to one in years, and they loved it. They were like two children caught up in the glittering, spell-binding fantasy world unique to the sawdust ring, eating popcorn and laughing loudly.

3

Parting

On Thursday, as arranged, they met Nomalizo and Roy at the ice rink. The four of them moved around the rink a couple of times but Thembi and Mduduzi soon put on speed and left the other two behind.

Thembi was delighted to find that her partner was a very competent skater. They held hands as they moved and then danced together, gradually getting bolder, trying out new steps as they adjusted to each other.

When they had finished Mduduzi suggested something to drink.

'You and Mduduzi seem very taken with each other,' said Nomalizo, as she and Thembi washed their hands in the cloakroom.

'Oh, he's wonderful!' exclaimed Thembi. 'We've been out together every night this week.' Nomalizo hugged her cousin and kissed her cheek.

'Thembi, I'm really happy for you. I've never seen you like this before. You're positively radiant. Be careful, though, Mduduzi's a mature man of the world and you've only known him for a few days. I'd hate to see you get hurt.'

'He won't hurt me. He feels the same way as I do. We enjoy being together and we have a lot in common. He's already very special to me and I've never felt about anyone else as I do about him,' said Thembi shyly. 'Oh, I'm so happy it frightens me,' she added. 'I feel almost as if I'm tempting fate to feel the way I do.' For a moment fear clouded her eyes and she shivered violently, her hands coming up to rub the goosebumps on her arms.

'Don't be silly, Thembi. Nobody can be too happy,' said Nomalizo sharply.

'I hope you're right. Come, let's go for that drink.'

They joined the men and the rest of the evening was spent laughing, skating and talking together.

'What would you like to do tomorrow night?' Mduduzi asked as they stood outside her front door.

'Would you like to spend the evening here?' she asked. 'How about coming to dinner?'

'There's nowhere I'd rather be.'

'My mother will probably serve up something which we've never had before. It happens every time we have guests!' laughed Thembi.

Mduduzi looked deeply into her eyes. 'Tonight has been very special to me, Thembi. You are beautiful and very graceful on the ice and I loved sharing your enjoyment. I felt proud and privileged just to see and be with you.' His eyes blazed with unspoken feeling and he took her in his arms and drew her close. He nuzzled her neck for a few moments before moving his lips, planting tiny kisses along her cheek, paying her silent homage before finally settling on her mouth.

The flame which ignited each time they touched immediately raged between them. Finally and reluctantly he released her. 'I'll see you tomorrow night,' he said, his voice harsh, his eyes caressing.

———— ♥ ————

Mduduzi arrived just after six-thirty the next evening. Thembi opened the door to him and he gave her a quick hug and a light kiss before they went into the lounge. His eyes followed her as she moved with the poise and grace of a dancer, totally unaware of how young and appealing she looked in her faded blue denim skirt, crisp white flower-embossed blouse and white sandals.

As Thembi had predicted, Dikeledi had prepared something unusual and the atmosphere at the table was relaxed and they talked about all sorts of things. Someone mentioned the number of recent international air disasters.

'The plane that crashed into the sea last Friday was the worst accident that SAA has suffered,' said Mduduzi. He glanced up and was arrested by the look of extreme anguish on Thembi's face.

'What's wrong?' he asked sharply.

Thembi swallowed then looked from him to her parents.

'I knew one of the passengers on that plane,' she replied quietly.

'Oh, Thembi, how dreadful,' said Dikeledi.

'Roberta was an Australian girl aged about twenty-three. She was visiting various countries gathering material for her Doctorate thesis in Political Science. She spent a week here and stayed for three of those days with Tony Richards, one of our assistant editors. Roberta spent most of Monday in our department, looking up files and talking to anyone who could spare the time. She was very pretty with a happy, outgoing nature.' Thembi did not raise her eyes from her plate all the time she was speaking.

'Today I typed a letter which Tony had written to her parents, telling them how she had spent her last few days. I can't remember when last I've cried so much. I could hardly see what I was doing. Tony has a wonderful way with words and if anything can ease their pain and grief, I think that letter will.'

There was a profound silence at the table, broken only by the sound of cutlery scraping on the plates.

When Thembi felt that the danger of her bursting into tears was past, she looked up and found Mduduzi's gaze trained on her face, an expression of immense compassion softening his features.

'How awful for that family,' said Dikeledi. 'When you hear of something like that it makes you realise just how fortunate you are. Now, how about dessert? I've made a strawberry mousse.'

The brisk, deliberate change of subject helped to dispel the feeling of gloom which the story had created.

Later the men retired to the lounge and the women followed once they had cleared everything away. They sat talking for about half an hour before Maliyeza and Dikeledi said they would be out for a while.

'I promised Naledi a couple of cakes for their sale tomorrow morning. Cripple Care are in desperate need of money for more wheel-chairs. We won't be long,' said Dikeledi.

After they had gone Mduduzi asked Thembi to play the piano for him.

She sat down and idly ran her fingers over the keys before settling down to play a medley from *Les Misérables* and *Phantom of the Opera*. She sang a few of the songs. Then she sang 'Deep in my Heart' from *The Student Prince*, unconsciously pouring out all the pent-up emotion of the past week. In the silence which followed the last clear, achingly sweet note she turned and looked at him.

He sat absolutely still; completely relaxed, his head lying on the backrest of the seat, eyes closed, hands clasped loosely behind his head. His eyes opened but he didn't move. Neither did she.

'Perfect.' He spoke only the one word but his eyes said it all. 'Come here. You're too far away,' he said huskily.

She removed her sandals then curled up next to him, tucking her feet in under her. He slid his arm around her shoulders and drew her close, his other hand covering hers.

'Thank you. That was beautiful.' There was silence for a few moments before he spoke again. 'I have to go to Cape Town tomorrow,' he said, looking down at their entwined fingers. Shocked, she sat perfectly still and he looked up at her. 'I can't help it, *mayi dali*. I don't want to go but these arrangements were made some time ago. I have some business to sort out which I think will take about two weeks and I promised my parents I'd spend these next two weekends with them.'

'Of course you must go,' she said, relaxing and giving his fingers a quick squeeze.

'What will you do while I'm away?'

'I'm going to be pretty busy next week. Apart from anything else, we have three choir rehearsals. Our choirmaster has been in Durban this week because his brother died. That's why I've been free every night. As the performance is only two months from now we will have to make up for lost time. Would you like me to get an extra ticket for you?' she asked shyly.

'Yes, please,' he replied, smiling at her. Then the smile faded from his lips and he looked at her with a troubled expression. 'I haven't seen my parents for about six months and my mother phoned last week to say that my father is having mild angina attacks, and they are both looking forward to seeing me tomorrow.'

'I'm sure they are,' she said softly.

His arm tightened as he pulled her to him. His face was close to hers and she could feel his warm breath on her cheek.

'I know I must go, but how the hell am I going to get through the next two weeks without you? I wish I could take you with me,' he said with suppressed violence. For a moment he looked as if he was in great pain. 'I can't bear the thought of leaving you. We've only known each other for a few days and yet to me it seems as if we've been together forever. I need you, Thembi. I need to know that you're there at the end of the day. I need to know that I will see you, touch you, hold you, kiss you,' he murmured desperately, his voice low and throbbing with emotion.

His hand moved from her shoulder to the nape of her neck and light pressure drew her forward to close the tiny gap between them as her lips met his. Her senses were spiralling out of control as they clung together exchanging greedy, famished kisses and when he raised his head he felt bereft and swiftly pulled it down again.

'Oh God, Thembi, I'm crazy about you,' he said roughly. 'I can't even think of you without going into a tailspin. I can't concentrate on my work. I can't sleep at night. I lie in bed fantasising about us and wishing you were with me and then, when I do eventually get to sleep I dream of nothing but you. You're like a fever in my blood for which there is only one cure.'

He pulled away abruptly and stood up, went to his jacket and, with hands that still shook, took a packet of cigarettes from his pocket. He lit one and inhaled deeply. He walked over to the window, opened the curtains and stood gazing out into the moonlit garden as he struggled to bring his thundering pulse under control.

The silence behind him was complete.

At last he turned around. Thembi was sitting as he had left her. He couldn't see her face but as he watched he saw tears drop on to her folded hands. With a smothered oath, he ground out his cigarette and with three steps was beside her. He crouched down on his haunches, then took her face in his hands, compelling her to look at him.

When he spoke it was very gently and very quietly.

'I'm sorry, *sithandwa*, beloved Thembi. Not for the world would I hurt or embarrass you.' Lifting her hands from her lap he brought them up to his mouth and held them there as he spoke. 'I'm sorry I let things get out of hand. Wanting you as I do and knowing that I must go away tomorrow is more than I can handle. Forgive me.'

'I am just as much to blame,' she replied, her voice no more than a thread of sound. 'I should have stopped you.'

Taking her head between his hands he brought it forward and kissed her forehead.

28

'My darling, the way I felt five minutes ago I doubt anyone could have stopped me,' he laughed, his voice not quite steady. 'It was only your innocence which did.'

He dried her eyes, stood up and, taking her hand in his, pulled her off the sofa.

'Come on woman, lead me to those games you spoke about,' he said gruffly.

The sudden switch from nerve-snapping tension to so ordinary a thing as games was so absurd that it earned him a wavery smile of gratitude as she went to the cupboard to get one out.

They had been playing for about half an hour when Dikeledi and Maliyeza returned.

After the game was over Thembi put a tape on the music deck and they all sat talking for a while.

It was still early when Mduduzi refused coffee and stood up, saying he had to go home and pack.

'I'm leaving on a very early flight for Cape Town tomorrow morning,' he explained to Maliyeza and Dikeledi. 'I have some business to attend to and I am going to spend some time with my parents.' While he was speaking Thembi fetched his jacket for him. He smiled his thanks, took his cheque book from the inside pocket, bent over a side table and wrote. The others watched him with varying degrees of puzzlement on their faces. Straightening up, he tore a page from the book and walked over to Dikeledi.

'I can't bake a cake and I won't be here to buy one tomorrow, so I'd like you to give this to your sister for me,' he said.

She looked down and her eyes widened in astonishment. She looked up at him and a delighted smile spread over her face.

'Oh, Mduduzi, thank you. This will probably pay for one wheel-chair by itself.' She reached up and kissed his cheek.

'Well, I must be going. I'll see you in about two weeks' time. Thanks for the dinner. Coming to see me off, Thembi?'

They went out together and walked to his car. They stood silently looking at each other, desperately trying to stave off the moment of parting. He made no attempt to get into the car. Instead he cradled her body within the strong shelter of his arms, rubbing his cheek against hers, his eyes closed.

'Dear God, I'm going to miss you. I'll phone you and let you know where I'll be staying.'

He looked down at her and the unconscious yearning in her glittering eyes and the passion of her slightly parted lips brought a muffled groan from him as he bent to meet her mouth in an achingly, sweet, lingering caress. They clung to each other in an effort to prolong this moment of sweet torment until at last he tore his mouth from hers and pushed her gently away.

Without another word he got into the car and drove away. Thembi stood watching, tears slowly trickling down her cheeks.

———————— ♥ ————————

The weekend dragged by. Thembi went shopping with her mother on Saturday morning and spent a couple of hours curled up on a lounger on the veranda in the afternoon. She took a book with her but found she could not concentrate so threw it down in disgust and lay staring at nothing in particular, seeing only a pair of brown eyes in a brown face.

She relived every minute they had spent together and knew that she was deeply, irrevocably in love with him, and needed him in her life as much as he had said he needed her.

She loved his gentleness, his strength; his protectiveness and possessiveness; his concern over his parents and his consideration for her feelings; his sense of humour and his delight in pleasing her. She loved everything about him.

Sunday was no better. She seemed to drift aimlessly about

the house, not able to settle to anything, not even her beloved music. She felt as if she had suddenly lost a limb. She was completely and utterly disorientated.

Just after tea the phone rang and she rushed to answer it.

'Is that you, Thembi?' asked Mduduzi in reply to her faint hello.

'Yes,' she breathed, her heart pounding, her hand shaking.

'Oh God, Thembi, I'm missing you.'

'I'm missing you too,' she replied, all her longing for him concentrated in those few words. 'How are your parents?'

'Not so good. I'm afraid the excitement of my arrival yesterday was too much for my father. It brought on another angina attack and, even though it was a mild one, it scared me. My mother is naturally worried but she doesn't say much. What have you been doing?'

'Nothing much except thinking of you,' she replied, unable to lie.

There was silence for a few seconds and then he spoke, his voice rough with emotion. 'Thank you, Thembi. I needed that. I must go now but I'll phone you tomorrow night. Sleep well, little one.'

Thembi felt more settled once she had heard from him and she told her parents about Mduduzi's father.

During the days that followed she felt like an automaton, eating, sleeping and going to work simply because she had to. The days, and evenings when she was at work or choir practice were not as bad as the nights she stayed home. They seemed endless, as she tossed and turned restlessly, waking unrefreshed and listless in the morning.

Mduduzi's phone calls on the nights she was not out were the only bright spots in an otherwise grey existence, but as time went on even they became strained and conversation was often stilted. It was obvious that the stress of their separation was affecting both of them.

'I'm pushing things through as quickly as I can,' he said

one night after he had been gone for just over a week. 'I'm trying to get through here in time to spend at least a part of Easter with you. I don't sleep at night, so rather than put myself through hell thinking of you I've been working till the early hours each morning. I can't wait to hold you in my arms again,' he said, his voice a soft caress. 'Don't make any arrangements for the weekend. We'll sort things out when I get back.'

'Oh Mduduzi, I miss you so much. I've felt little better than a zombie ever since you left. Please hurry home.' It was a cry from the heart and she did not try to hide her feelings.

On Wednesday the newspaper carried a story about a family who had a very bleak long weekend to look forward to. The father had been out of work for two months and a picture of him and his wife and their five children, all dressed in clothes that were patched and looked very like charity hand-outs, appeared with the story.

'It's a real tear-jerker,' said Tony Richards when he saw Thembi reading the report.

'I agree,' she answered wryly. 'The only thing is that reading this you'd think they are the only family who are having a rough time. Nothing has been said of the hundreds of people who have recently lost their jobs or others who have been unemployed for months.'

'I agree, but I bet the story will prick quite a few consciences before this night is out,' he replied. 'It will be interesting to see public reaction to it.' They found out early the next morning.

When Thembi arrived at work there were a number of packages on her desk and by ten o'clock the surface was covered. There were cheques and envelopes with money, parcels of clothing, biscuits, sweets and chocolates, cakes, groceries, meat, fruit and vegetables. By midday every inch of available space was filled and nobody else could get into her office.

Her routine work was shared between the two junior secretaries while Thembi contacted the Social Welfare and Red Cross. Then she helped them clear everything away for distribution among the needy. It was half past three before everything had been removed and Thembi felt as if she had been flattened by a steam roller. She was sitting at her desk with her eyes closed, her fingers moving restlessly over her forehead to try to ease a niggling headache when her phone rang.

'Hello,' she said listlessly.

'Thembi? Is that you?'

'Mduduzi!' she cried in delight, then frowned in consternation. 'Is something wrong?'

'No, *mayi fohloza*, there's nothing wrong. I'm at the airport in Cape Town and have managed to get a seat on a flight leaving in an hour's time. Will you meet me at Jan Smuts at about six o'clock?'

'Of course I will,' she replied joyously.

'I can't wait to be with you again,' he said, his voice rough with emotion.

They said goodbye and Thembi slowly replaced the receiver, feeling the stress and tension of the day draining away at the prospect of being with him again.

She phoned home and told her mother she was going to meet Mduduzi and that they would probably be home for dinner, although she didn't know when.

She cleared up the odd bits of outstanding work in her office then went to the cloakroom where she swallowed a couple of pills to ease her headache, brushed her hair and applied a light lip gloss, and was satisfied with the result. All signs of strain had vanished.

4

Commitment

At the airport Thembi waited with mingled excitement and impatience. It was quite dark outside when the plane landed and, unable to recognise the passengers on the tarmac, she stepped away from the window – and there he was, striding through from the arrivals area, smiling broadly.

Words were unnecessary as he folded her in his arms. She revelled in his strength. Her arms tightened eagerly about him, expressing her joy at having him back. He held her firmly against him, eyes closed, head buried in the curve of her neck, as he enjoyed the feel of her, the smell of the delicate perfume she wore, absorbing her very essence, and she was overwhelmed by the impact of his masculinity.

He moved his head to kiss her. Nothing else existed for either of them as they silently communicated their hunger for each other.

'I hope you don't mind, I told my mother I'd bring you back with me for dinner,' she said, as they drove away from the airport.

'Thank you, I'd like that. But would you mind if we stopped off at my apartment first? I'll leave my luggage there and follow you in my car.'

When she was in the car he settled himself behind the wheel. He drove swiftly and competently and soon they were turning into the underground parking of a high-rise block of luxury apartments. As they stepped inside number 89 Mduduzi closed the door and flicked on the light switch.

'Come here,' he growled impatiently, dropping his suitcase and turning her towards him. With one swift movement he anchored her to him as he brought his head down to claim her lips with a devastating, raw urgency which ignited in her a fierce and primitive response, releasing all the frustration and yearning of the past fortnight.

'Never again, Thembi,' he said in low, intense tones. 'I never want to go anywhere without you, ever again. I know we only met a short while ago but I have been waiting all my life for you. I knew you were the one on the night of your party and the past three weeks have merely confirmed it. This time away from you has been sheer hell. I love you, *mayi dali*, more than I'll ever be able to tell you. You are the other half of me, and together we form one perfect unit. Do you understand what I'm trying to say?'

'Of course I understand. Being your other half, how could I not?' she replied simply. She looked at him with a smile radiant with joy, her face suffused with love. 'I love you, Mduduzi, so very, very much,' she whispered, her fingers tracing the outline of his face as if trying to imprint it forever on her memory. 'Without you I simply cannot function properly any more. I need you to make my life complete. I am yours, body and soul, *sithandwa*.' Her voice throbbed with passionate intensity and there was no doubting her sincerity.

He closed his eyes and swallowed, then slowly expelled the breath he had been holding. With an exultant cry he crushed her in his arms and, with a savagery which was almost frightening, his mouth found hers in an explosion of unbridled passion. The surging rhythm of his heartbeat echoed her own in the emotionally super-charged atmosphere.

'Marry me, Thembi. Come and live here and share my home, my bed, my life and my future with me?' he asked softly.

'Oh yes, I want to be your wife more than anything else in the world,' she replied without hesitation, tears of happiness filling her eyes.

His arms cradled her protectively, almost reverently, as

though they held something infinitely fragile and precious and hers held him close as they sealed their commitment to each other with an achingly tender caress.

Reluctantly they drew apart and, taking her hand, he led her down a single step into the lounge. As they passed a table lamp Mduduzi flicked the switch and the room was bathed in a warm glow of soft light. He took off his jacket, put his hand into the inside pocket, brought out a small velvet box and snapped open the lid. Inside lay a diamond solitaire, flanked on either side by diamond chips set in a delicate leaf design.

'Oh,' she breathed, raising her eyes to his, an expression of awed bemusement on her face. 'It's beautiful.' His eyes held hers with a look of boundless tenderness which brought fresh tears to her eyes.

'Don't cry, *sithandwa*, please.'

'If we're to be married you'll have to get used to the idea that I cry when I'm happy or very emotional as well as when I'm sad,' she replied tremulously.

Taking her left hand in his he gently pushed the ring over the knuckle of the third finger. 'With this ring I put my heart and love into your keeping. Guard them well, my love,' he said with deep sincerity, kissing her fingers as he spoke.

'I will. I promise.'

'We won't have to wait too long,' he said confidently, as he showed her round the luxurious apartment. 'We are going to be married just as soon as your mother can arrange it. I realise that your parents are going to want a large affair and I want to see you come to me in a wreath and veil, with all the trappings of a young bride.' As he spoke he grew very serious. 'I love you with every fibre of my being and I can't begin to tell you what having your love means to me,' he said, caressing her cheek, as they stood outside his bedroom.

They turned and walked into the room which was a

tranquil study of beige and varying shades of brown. A very masculine room, austere in its neatness.

'There's an en suite bathroom through there,' he said, pointing at the door.

Thembi stood beside him and looked at the double bed. Watching her keenly he saw the expression on her face and answered her unspoken question.

'No, *sithandwa*, no woman has ever shared that bed with me. I am not saying I have lived the life of a monk. I'm over thirty and a normal, healthy man. There have been occasions when I've taken what has been offered, but I've never loved any woman as I love you and I give you my solemn vow that I will never be unfaithful to you, or knowingly hurt you in any way. I love you, and I've never said that to anyone before.'

Thembi flung her arms around his neck and rained tiny kisses over his face, finally settling on his mouth.

'Thank you,' she whispered. 'It's no wonder I love you as I do. I've never felt about anyone as I do about you and that is why I've never been to bed with anyone. I've never wanted to – until now.' A delicate flush warmed her cheeks as she spoke. 'Oh, Mduduzi, hold me tight. Don't ever let me go.' Her passionate pleas and her words inflamed him and, as they clung to each other in mindless rapture, he realised the danger they were courting.

'Whoa there, my girl,' he said thickly. 'I think it's time we got out of here.'

She smiled mistily at him and they walked out of the room with their arms around each other and headed towards the entrance hall.

'Before we go would you mind if I phoned my parents? I've told them all about you and that I was hoping to marry you so our news won't come as a surprise,' he said.

She stood next to him as he spoke to his mother then she spoke to his parents. She was very shy at first, but they soon put her at ease. Mduduzi then spoke to his father and in response to something his father said he gave a loud laugh of pure happiness, then rang off.

'He says he can't wait to meet the girl who has finally harnessed me,' he chuckled. 'He also said they'd let Lindi know. I told you about her, didn't I?' he asked, his head cocked slightly to one side, one eyebrow raised questioningly.

'Yes, you did.'

'I wish I could be a fly on the wall when she hears about us,' he said, grinning. 'The last time I saw her she wanted to know when I was going to settle down and start a family. Very impertinent she was, telling me she thought I was leaving it a bit late to get going. Anyway, I told her I was waiting for my perfect partner. She told me to grow up and realise that fairy stories are for children! I can't wait to see her face when she meets you,' he said, linking his arms loosely about her waist and kissing the tip of her nose. 'Because our fairy story does have a happy ending, doesn't it, *mayi dali*?'

They left the apartment and when they reached Thembi's home she pulled him impatiently by the hand and hurried him into the lounge. Standing together, the words tumbled joyously from her as she told her parents they were engaged. She then threw herself into her mother's arms before turning to her father to be hugged by him.

Mduduzi saw Dikeledi open her mouth to speak and Maliyeza silently shake his head at her. Mduduzi mouthed a silent thank you to the man who would soon be his father-in-law. They both understood Dikeledi's concern at the short time they had known each other.

They drank a toast to welcome Mduduzi to the family with Thembi telling her parents all about Mduduzi's home.

Later in the evening as they sat talking Mduduzi looked at

Thembi who was sitting quietly, rubbing her forehead and frowning slightly.

'What's wrong?' he asked.

'Nothing. I have a slight headache, that's all. It's probably a result of all the excitement tonight and the chaos at work today. I took a couple of tablets just before I left work but I will go and take some more just now.'

She told them about the news story and its consequences, but he sensed that she wasn't admitting to how bad her headache was. He left soon afterwards, saying that he had to unpack and had a few things to sort out while they were still fresh in his mind.

Before leaving he cradled her gently in his arms, kissing her deeply but briefly.

'Goodnight, *sithandwa*. Thank you for making this one of the happiest and most memorable days of my life. Go to bed now and don't forget to take something for that headache. I'll see you tomorrow morning. I'm coming to lunch and we have a lot of planning to do.'

She said goodnight to her parents, took some tablets and crawled into bed, grateful for the darkness as she lay quietly on her back waiting for the pills to take effect. Blinding pain such as she had never before experienced pounded through her head, and she found when she put her hand up over her eyes that her throbbing temples were very painful to touch.

By the next morning she felt much better although there was still a dull ache over her eyes but she managed to keep the pain at bay by taking pain-killers periodically throughout the day. As promised, Mduduzi spent the day with her.

A private family celebration was arranged for Saturday night and Thembi's radiance and joy reached out and infected them all.

Dressed in a soft, flowing dress of turquoise chiffon that emphasised her curves, Thembi walked proudly beside her fiancé, her hand tucked possessively into the crook of his arm, his smart suit and white silk shirt accentuating his good looks. The evening was filled with laughter and happiness but the headache which had been worrying Thembi returned, and as the evening progressed she found it more and more difficult to cope with the pain. She was also beginning to feel sick.

During a lull in the conversation Mduduzi put out his hand to cover hers. 'Good God!' he exclaimed. 'Your hand is on fire. Are you all right?'

Tears welled up into her eyes and she shook her head, closing her eyes. 'No,' she whispered. 'That headache has come back and I feel as if my head is about to split wide open. Pain-killers aren't helping any more.'

Within minutes he had called for the bill, assuring everyone that the dinner had been superb but that unfortunately the young lady wasn't feeling well and they wanted to get her home to bed.

Dikeledi climbed into the back of the car and Mduduzi insisted that Thembi get in beside her. She went into her mother's arms and laid her head, as she had done so many times in her childhood, on the loving and comforting shoulder while tears coursed uncontrollably down her cheeks.

As soon as they reached home Maliyeza phoned the doctor who said he would come immediately. Dikeledi went to prepare Thembi's bed while Mduduzi sat and held her in his arms, wiping the perspiration from her hot, damp forehead and tears from her cheeks.

'I'm so sorry I spoilt our beautiful evening,' she cried brokenly.

'Oh my love,' he replied, a catch in his voice, 'you have nothing to be sorry about.' He put his lips to her forehead in an effort to comfort her. She was burning up with fever and a deep, very real fear began to grow within him.

Dikeledi came back and she and Mduduzi led Thembi

through to her bedroom, where her mother helped her undress and get into bed.

Mduduzi went back to the lounge and he and Maliyeza sat quietly together, each intent on his own thoughts as they waited for the doctor to arrive. They did not wait long. He went straight through to Thembi's room.

Mduduzi sat chewing distractedly on the knuckle of one finger while the anxiety and fear that gripped him showed clearly in his eyes.

Maliyeza sat and smoked his cigarette, the clenching and unclenching of his hand as he gripped the armrest of his chair the only sign of his acute agitation, as he waited for the doctor to finish his examination.

'I've given her a sedative and something to help bring down her temperature,' said the doctor as he walked into the lounge. 'She should sleep through the night but I am not happy about her temperature. It is quite high. I will come back early tomorrow morning and see how she is. Call me if you need me before then.'

He left soon afterwards and Dikeledi walked over to Mduduzi and put her hand on his head.

'Would you like to sleep here tonight? Maliyeza can lend you some pyjamas and we always have spare toothbrushes.' She smiled understandingly as she spoke.

He looked up at her and took her hand in his.

'Thank you. I don't think I could bear to be alone tonight. Are you sure it's no trouble?'

'None at all,' she replied.

Mduduzi took off his jacket and tie and sat on the side of the bed, his hands hanging loosely between his knees, his thoughts in a turmoil as he gazed unseeingly at a spot on the carpet. Pictures of his beloved Thembi flashed through his mind. The places they had been to together, her moving gracefully over the ice as she skated for him, her radiant smile when she told him she loved him, her joy as she gazed

41

at her engagement ring. Then finally, every detail indelibly engraved on his memory, the look of suffering on her face when she was compelled to succumb to the unbearable pain which she had tried so valiantly to hide.

He stood up and restlessly started pacing the floor. After a while he quietly went through to her room. He drew up a chair next to her bed and sat silently looking at her. By the light of the night lamp which Dikeledi had left burning, he saw that her skin shone with moisture.

Very quietly he went to the kitchen and bathroom then, armed with a bowl of tepid water and a face cloth, he returned and gently started to wipe the perspiration from her face.

She was very restless, despite the sedative.

'Oh God, please let her get well soon. I love her so much,' he prayed silently.

He never left her side and at about four o'clock Dikeledi came in and found him still sitting in the chair with his head resting on the side of the bed, Thembi's hand clasped in his. He was fast asleep and she was resting peacefully. Dikeledi shook him gently and told him to go to bed, that she would keep watch for the remainder of the night.

He went to his room, undressed and tumbled into bed.

It seemed to him that he had just put his head on the pillow when he was woken by a scream which sent him bolting through to Thembi's room. He found Dikeledi, tears pouring down her cheeks, trying to support her daughter who was struggling to get out of bed. Every movement brought pain-induced screams from her and she was crying helplessly.

Mduduzi took her weight as he supported her, helping to lift her up.

'Do you want to go to the bathroom?' he asked.

She nodded her head slightly and he picked her up and carried her, while spasms of pain continually racked her body. She bit her lip, trying to stop herself from crying out.

Between them Mduduzi and Dikeledi helped her back to bed. She complained that her neck and back felt stiff and sore.

Maliyeza, who had also been woken by Thembi's cries, came into the room.

'I've phoned the doctor and he's coming right away.'

Mduduzi went to his room and got dressed. He met Dikeledi at the door of Thembi's room and she told him that the doctor was in there with her.

He was with her for only a few minutes. He went to the telephone and after making his calls, he asked Dikeledi to pack a suitcase for Thembi.

'I'm moving her into hospital straight away,' said the doctor.

Within ten minutes an ambulance had arrived and Thembi, now unconscious, was taken away.

'I'm going to the hospital now,' said the doctor. 'We will get tests going immediately and I'll let you know as soon as we do what the problem is. I'm putting her into isolation until we know what we're dealing with so you won't be able to visit her just yet.'

5

Tragedy

Days of anxiety followed for those who loved her and for Thembi it was a time of bouts of unbearable pain and intense confusion mixed with periods of oblivion. All telephone calls to the hospital received the same cautious, non-committal reply – she was being kept sedated.

On the Thursday following her admission to hospital the doctor phoned Maliyeza at work.

'You, your wife and Mr Mkhize may see Thembi for a while this evening. I've had her moved to a private ward and I'd like to speak to the three of you after you've seen her. If I'm not there at the end of visiting time, please wait for me.'

'Thanks, doctor. How is she?'

'The fever has gone and her temperature is just about normal. She's lost quite a bit of weight and her headaches have gone, but I'll see you tonight and we can go into the details then.'

Maliyeza phoned Dikeledi and Mduduzi then sat chewing his lips as he thought about the conversation he had just had with the doctor. Something about it troubled him but he could not put his finger on it.

He and his wife arrived at the hospital to find Mduduzi waiting for them. The sister on duty showed them to Thembi's ward and Mduduzi stood back to allow her parents to go first.

He was profoundly thankful that he had.

The eyes which moved quickly from one to the other of her visitors were dull and sunken. Her hair had been brushed back and emphasised the gaunt outlines of her face.

Mduduzi felt his stomach and fists clench as he strove desperately not to show how shocked he was. After her parents had kissed her they stood back and he went to her bedside.

'Hello, *mayi dali*,' he whispered, barely able to control his voice. 'I've missed you so much and because we love you we have all been very worried about you.' He kissed her gently on the lips, taking her hand in one of his. He cupped one of her cheeks in his other hand and she turned her head and kissed his palm. He could not have spoken a single word at that moment had his life depended on it.

'I'm so glad to see you all. While I was ill I kept calling but you never came. Every time I woke up I wanted you to be here but you never were,' she said petulantly. 'Then the nurses and the doctor explained that I've been very ill and that you were not allowed to see me. But I'm better now and you're here,' she added with a faint smile as she squeezed his hand.

That smile was a pitifully heart-breaking attempt and they all had to swallow a lump in their throats while she continued to speak, 'Thank you for the flowers. They arrived soon after I was moved to this ward.'

Two bowls of flowers stood on the locker beside her bed; one with pink carnations and the other with roses and proteas.

'How are you feeling, *dudu wami*?' asked Maliyeza, using his pet childhood name for her. 'As Mduduzi has said, we've all been very worried. The whole family sends their love.'

'Thank you. I'm feeling much better and I'm fine as long as I don't move. Then it's very painful,' she replied with a smile which did not quite reach her eyes. 'But thank God that headache has gone. I thought I'd go mad, the way it was throbbing.'

The visit was a strain on them all; on Thembi because she was getting very tired; on her loved ones because it was becoming more and more difficult to speak and act naturally when they were all trying not to show the shock and fear they were feeling. At last Mduduzi could stand it no longer.

'I think we should go now. You look as if you're going to drop off to sleep at any moment,' he said with a smile which he dredged up from some hidden reserve of strength. 'We'll be here tomorrow afternoon and every minute we're allowed to see you until you come home.'

'I am tired, but very happy now that I've seen you. I love you all so much.' They could hardly hear her words, as her eyes closed and she drifted off to sleep, her face peaceful in repose.

They quietly left the ward and went into the waiting room where they found the doctor.

'I see her appearance has come as a shock to you, despite my warning. Don't worry, she'll regain the weight she's lost. That is the least of our worries and there is no way to soften what I have to say, I'm afraid, so I'll be blunt. We have carried out extensive tests and we are positive of our diagnosis. Thembi has contracted polio.'

'Polio!' burst from Mduduzi in stunned disbelief.

'Oh my God,' said Maliyeza, his voice anguished.

Dikeledi said nothing. Her hand shot up to cover her mouth and tears filled her eyes as she turned to her husband, whose arms closed about her, giving what comfort he could while suffering from shock himself.

'But wasn't Thembi immunised against it?' asked Mduduzi in bewilderment.

'Yes, she was,' replied the doctor. 'Polio is a virus. How it is transmitted we don't yet know. It strikes indiscriminately and although it's well under control these days, there are still those million-to-one chances which occur over which we have no control. The only consolation is that we believe she will not be badly crippled. Her legs appear to be the only limbs affected, her right one more so than the left. Of course, we could be wrong, but present indications are that with intensive physiotherapy and her full co-operation, she should be left with little more than a weakness in that leg. It will take time and all the patience, love and support you can give her.

'I'm having her moved to a convalescent home tomorrow, where we can give concentrated and undivided attention to her recovery. Visitors are allowed only on Wednesday evenings and in the afternoons and evenings over the weekends. We do this because the effort the patients are expected to put into their treatment is extremely tiring and it is essential that we go into top gear from the word go to prevent muscle shrinkage.

'I'm handing her over to Mr Carlstein, a brilliant orthopaedic specialist, who has agreed to take her as a patient. I knew there was no need to ask your permission as we all have Thembi's interests at heart. I'm going in to tell her now. We will leave her in the private ward tonight as she is bound to be very upset. Don't worry, though, we will give her something to make her sleep through the night.' Although his voice was matter-of-fact, his eyes conveyed his deep compassion.

'Thank you for looking after our girl for us,' said Maliyeza. He turned to the other two. 'Come along, I think we'd best leave now. There is nothing more we can do here.'

———— ❤ ————

The next morning Thembi was moved to the convalescent home. She was put into a private ward so that she could adjust to the changes more easily. She was pleased to find that her flowers had been brought with her and every time she looked at them she felt less lonely and isolated from those she loved.

Jean Grant, a woman of about forty, was the physiotherapist assigned to work with Thembi. Well-built, always smiling and jovial, attractive in a warm, homely sort of way, with short-cropped, naturally curly brown hair and hands which were extremely strong but could be infinitely gentle with someone in pain, she was very patient and loving. She saw each new patient as a personal challenge. She was determined to get Thembi back on her feet but knew from years of experience that a long, difficult road lay ahead of them.

When the treatment started she kept Thembi in her bed and worked in the privacy of her ward. Thembi struggled valiantly to do what was asked of her but found it impossible to move her legs or feet without some help. Then, as a result, she suffered excruciating pain and maddening pins and needles in the muscles which were gently being coaxed back to life.

Each time Thembi was reduced to tears and ready to give up, Jean would encourage and spur her on to try again, and again, and yet again. She would have to harden her heart to the pitiful sight of Thembi, with tears of frustration in her eyes and her teeth gritted in fierce determination, trying to get her legs to move, only to find that no matter how much effort she put into it, they simply would not respond.

The first time Thembi had to face her loved ones after being admitted to the home was probably the most traumatic experience any of them had ever endured.

It was decided that Dikeledi and Maliyeza would go and see her in the afternoon on visiting days and Mduduzi would go in the evening. They felt that it would be better not to crowd her.

When her parents were shown to her ward they found Thembi very weepy. Being in a private ward she was able to let herself go and did not even try to put on a brave face for them.

'Where's Mduduzi?' she asked, after greeting them.

Maliyeza explained their arrangement and the reason for it. 'Besides, Naledi and her family will be coming sometimes

48

and we probably won't all be allowed in at the same time if there are too many of us. Now then, tell us how you are.'

She looked at him disbelievingly for a moment and then her face crumpled.

'I'm going to be crippled and I can't walk,' she cried hysterically. 'You know that, so why ask me how I am? How do you expect me to be?' she demanded, then burst into tears.

'Stop that immediately,' thundered Maliyeza. She obeyed instinctively, though she gazed at him with a wounded look in her tear-drenched eyes, and choked back a sob.

Without giving her a chance to say anything, he went on speaking, and even though his voice was softer there was an unmistakable thread of steel running through it. She recognised what she had always secretly called his 'no nonsense voice'.

'Don't you *ever* let me hear you say that again, do you understand me?' he clipped out, his jaw clenched as he strove to control his anger. 'You are *not* going to be crippled and you *will* walk again. That is why you are here – and don't you ever forget it!'

His eyes shone with all the love in the world and his features softened as he took her hands in his. Dikeledi sat quietly by, trusting him implicitly to find the right words to help their child when she needed them so desperately. Never before had his dependability been more evident as he faced what was probably the greatest challenge of his life.

'We have spoken to Mr Carlstein and he has been very frank with us. If this had happened to you twenty or thirty years ago, you would undoubtedly have been severely handicapped, but with today's medicines and physiotherapy, together with your full co-operation, there is no reason why you should not recover the full use of your legs. The fact that you were immunised should save you from severe damage, but there is a strong chance that you will be left with a weakness in one or possibly even both your legs, particularly your ankles. I presume Mr Carlstein has already told you all this but we want you to know and believe that your mother, Mduduzi and I are behind you every step of the way – and I mean that literally.' When he had finished speaking, he bent down and kissed her cheek, cupping her face in the palms of his hands.

'Thank you, Baba. I'm sorry I behaved so badly just now, but I am so terribly frightened.' Her lips trembled and she blew her nose fiercely to try to stop the tears from spilling over.

'I know, and we understand. Now tell us what's happened to you since we saw you the other night.'

They talked for a while and she told them about Jean and the treatment she had been given so far.

Thembi was emotionally and physically exhausted and long before the visiting hour was over she had drifted off to sleep. Her parents sat sadly beside her bed for a while then quietly got up and left.

By the time Mduduzi went to her that evening he had himself well under control. He had spoken to Maliyeza before leaving his apartment so was fairly well prepared for what to expect.

'Mduduzi,' she cried as he shut the door of the ward behind him. She held out her arms to him and he went swiftly across the floor, bent over and kissed her while sliding his arms under her and holding her close. She put her arms around his neck and held on to him tightly while she sobbed out her misery.

He let her cry for a few minutes then gently disentangled her arms from his neck, took her hands into his and slowly lifted himself away from her. He gazed down at her unhappy face.

'Please try not to cry any more, *sithandwa*. It won't take much to have me in tears as well and how do you think it would look if one of the nurses came in and found us both crying like over-grown school kids?' he teased, trying to coax a smile from her.

His reward was a rather wobbly one, but a smile nevertheless.

'I'm sorry,' she gulped. She looked at him with eyes pleading for reassurance. 'I'm so afraid,' she whispered.

'I know, *mayi dali*, and believe me we have all been afraid,' he said. 'It is a strange thing about human beings. We go to church and profess our faith in God's everlasting love. Then when faced with trouble we are full of fear and seem to lose faith not only in God but the doctors and nursing staff and their skills as well.'

By the time he had finished speaking she had managed to pull herself together and he gave a small sigh of relief.

He looked down at her and smiled. 'That's better,' he said, using his foot to hook a chair towards him, settling himself next to her bed, never leaving go of her hands for a second. 'Now tell me what's been happening to you. Every detail,' he added.

She told him what she had told her parents earlier in the day and as time went on she felt calmer and he felt reassured.

'I phoned my parents,' he said, just before it was time for him to go. 'Naturally they were very upset but send their love. Thank God I was honestly able to tell them the doctor is very optimistic about your recovery.' He cupped her face in his hands as he gazed intently into her eyes. 'I have never been so scared in all my life as I was on Thursday night. I love you with all my heart and I want you to remember that always.' His voice was rough with emotion.

The bell rang to show the end of visiting time and he stood up, kissing her lingeringly on the lips, then on the fingers that clung to his hands. 'I'll see you tomorrow evening. Sleep well, my Thembi.'

Sunday was very much the same as the day before and

Thembi felt almost relieved when she settled down for the night. She was finding it a strain not to let her anxiety and fear get the better of her when her loved ones were there, and they felt the same.

On Monday morning she was put into a wheel-chair and taken to the physiotherapy department. Jean took her straight to the cubicle where they were to work and although there were other patients working on different apparatus in the room she did not stop, merely greeted them with a smile and a cheery word as they passed by.

As usual, Thembi found it a difficult and painful ordeal that seemed to go on forever, without anything apparent to show for it by the time she was taken, exhausted, back to her bed, just before lunch time.

On her bed was a large package. Jean helped her open it and gave a delighted chuckle as Thembi lifted out a teddy bear. Around his neck, tied like a bib, was a message: 'My name is Mduduzi II and I am very lonely. Can I cuddle up with you?'

'Who is Mduduzi I?' asked Jean, still laughing.

'My fiancé,' replied Thembi shyly.

Jean looked perplexed as her eyes rested on Thembi's bare hands.

'He took my ring to keep it safe for me when I came here. I've lost so much weight it was very loose and I was afraid I'd lose it,' Thembi explained.

'Well, come along my girl, let's pop you into bed so you can cuddle your teddy.'

She left and as Thembi lay hugging her gift she wept silently, her longing for Mduduzi and a large dose of self-pity all mixed up in the tears she shed.

Soon after lunch Sister Dlamini came into the ward. Strad-dling her hip, with tiny arms around her neck, was a little girl. Thembi saw a mass of golden blonde curls and two large, blue eyes peering at her inquisitively before the little face was buried shyly in the sister's neck.

'Come along, Mandy, you're not really shy. I want you to meet Thembi,' said Sister Dlamini coaxingly.

Mandy slowly turned her head sideways, keeping it close to the sister's face, and solemnly regarded Thembi for a few seconds before smiling enchantingly and putting her arms out to go to her.

'You little darling,' chuckled the sister, seating Mandy carefully on Thembi's bed. Mandy spied the teddy bear and immediately held out her arms for it. Thembi gave it to her and Mandy hugged it and started to kiss it.

Thembi laughed happily and Sister Dlamini joined in. She shook her head, smiling affectionately at the little girl.

'Everybody in the home adores this little mite,' she said.

Thembi looked at Mandy and the smile faded from her face. For the first time she noticed the little girl's legs and was horrified when she realised that they were both in callipers and on her tiny feet she wore boots.

'What's wrong with her?' she whispered, appalled.

'She was born with club feet,' was the matter-of-fact reply. 'Her treatment started almost from the day she was born. We have been told that she was in splints and plaster until about six months ago when she was operated on and her feet were straightened. Then she was put into plaster again until about two months ago, and has been with us ever since. She is learning to walk and we are very proud of her progress. May I leave her with you for a few minutes? Little Sipho next door seemed a bit restless when I passed there just now and I'd like to go and check up on him. I won't be long.' Without waiting for a reply, she walked out of the ward.

Mandy was hugging the teddy bear and crooning softly to it. She turned to Thembi and, still holding fast on to the teddy, snuggled up to her. Thembi's arms instinctively tightened around her.

After a while Mandy wriggled and sat up. Gravely she looked at Thembi. 'What's his name?' she asked, her eyes solemnly studying Thembi's face.

'Mduduzi,' was the husky reply.

'Duzi,' repeated the little girl. 'Mandy likes Duzi,' she stated emphatically. 'Mandy likes Thembi,' she added coyly.

Thembi laughed delightedly and hugged her and Mandy chuckled in response.

Sister Dlamini came back into the room and smiled, a satisfied gleam in her eyes.

'Come along, imp, it's time for your nap,' she said, lifting Mandy up into her arms.

'Mandy wants Duzi,' she said, lips pouting.

'If Duzi is the teddy bear, I think we should leave him here to look after Thembi. You can come and visit him again tomorrow,' she promised.

Smiling happily, Mandy went with her and Thembi lay back, absentmindedly cuddling her teddy bear, thinking about little Mandy and all she must have suffered so far in her short life.

6

Adjustment

The next morning, just as she was finishing her breakfast, Thembi heard a sound at the door of her ward.

Seated in a wheel-chair, with a rug thrown carelessly over his legs, sat a red-haired boy of about twelve, looking intently at her.

'Hello,' she said, her face as solemn as his.

'How long have you been here? What's your name?' he asked in a gruff voice, not wasting time but getting straight to the heart of his interest. His gaze was unwavering.

'Since last Friday, and I'm Thembi,' she replied.

'I'm Keith. What's wrong with you?'

Thembi was starting to feel a bit uncomfortable under the boy's direct, unfaltering gaze, but she was determined not to be beaten in a battle of wills.

'Polio. What's wrong with you?'

'I lost a leg in a motor accident but I've never met anyone with polio before. What *is* polio?' he asked.

Thembi was suddenly struck by the absurdity of the situation and started laughing with an abandonment she had not felt for a long time. An answering grin began to spread over the boy's face and, bending forward in his chair, he propelled himself swiftly forward until he was next to her bed.

'What is polio?' he repeated.

Thembi told him briefly and he listened with a look of deep concentration on his face.

'I guess you're luckier than I am,' he said gravely.

'What do you mean?' asked Thembi.

'You have two legs. I only have one now.'

With that he threw back the rug and Thembi saw that one

pyjama leg had been neatly folded up and pinned into
position while the other one covered his remaining limb, on
the foot of which Keith wore a brown leather slipper.

'I'm so sorry, Keith. Thank you for showing me.' Secretly
her heart was wrung with pity but she knew that she must
not let her feelings show. 'How old are you?' she asked.

'Twelve,' he replied, then losing any reserve, he burst into
speech. 'Oh, Thembi, I wish you could see what my new
leg's going to be like. It's going to be super. They are busy
making it for me now and Doc Carlstein showed me one like
it and it's got a spring in the knee and also in the ankle. He
says when I've learnt to walk with it nobody will even know
it's not my real one,' he rushed on excitedly, hardly pausing
for breath. 'He says my Dad will be very proud of me.'

'I'm sure he will be,' she replied. 'And your mother too.'

'My Mom's dead. She died when I was very small and I
don't remember her at all. Dad was in the accident, too. He
was driving.'

'Was he hurt as well?' she asked cautiously, not wanting
to cause him pain.

'Oh, he's OK,' was the gruff reply. 'He had some cuts on
his hands and face and he hurt his wrist. But my leg was
trapped and I had to be cut free from the car. The doctor at
the hospital said it was a real mess and wouldn't be any use
to me any more and they would make me a new one.' This
last piece of information was imparted with all the gruesome
relish and self-importance so often displayed by small boys.

'So there you are, Keith,' said Jean, coming into the room.
'Everybody is looking for you so you'd best scoot back quickly
before you land yourself in trouble again.' She frowned as if
trying to remember something. 'I think I saw Miss Jones with
a spanking new leg in her hands just now,' she said, a
twinkle in her eyes.

Keith gave a great whoop of joy then spun his wheel-chair
round and headed for the door, furiously wheeling himself

as he went. 'I'll see you later, Thembi,' he shouted, and was gone.

'What a little scamp he is, but you can't help loving him,' said Jean. 'He has so much courage. His father is a very pleasant man, but he is suffering dreadfully from guilt because of the accident, although it was not his fault. They were caught in heavy traffic one afternoon. An impatient idiot coming from the opposite direction pulled out of his lane to overtake and Keith's father suddenly found himself confronted by this car heading straight for him. He swerved and unfortunately went down an embankment and the car rolled. Keith's leg got trapped in the wreckage and it was too mangled to save. The other motorist never even stopped,' said Jean bitterly. 'And now, young lady, it's time to start working.'

After a gruelling two-hour stint, Thembi could take no more. Jean, too, was exhausted.

'How about a swim?' she asked.

'A swim?' asked Thembi eagerly. 'Where?'

'We have an indoor, slightly heated pool if you're interested.'

'Oh yes, please,' said Thembi excitedly, then her face fell. 'How am I going to get in and out of the water?' she asked dully. 'And, I haven't got a costume.'

Jean shook her head. 'Oh Thembi, don't be such a defeatist,' she said. 'There is a ramp instead of steps leading into the pool and you can slide down and up again on your bottom, using your arms to push yourself along – there's nothing wrong with *them*.' Seeing the unhappy look in Thembi's eyes, she bent down and hugged her. 'I'm sorry honey, I didn't mean to hurt your feelings. Come, I'll get into the water with you and you can have your choice of costumes. There's a room full of them.'

They spent the next hour or so in the pool, Jean helping

her to try to get as much movement as possible in her legs. Thembi found that she felt much less pain in the water.

When they arrived back in her ward she found a parcel on her bed with a compact radio/cassette recorder, headphones and a dozen tapes in it. They were all her favourites from the shows from which she had played and sung numbers for Mduduzi. His message was simple. 'I love you. Think of me when you listen to these.'

———— ♥ ————

'Look Thembi,' shouted Keith later that afternoon, excitedly wheeling himself swiftly into her ward then stopping abruptly when he realised she was not alone. He blushed vividly.

'I'm sorry, I didn't know you had visitors,' he muttered gruffly. 'I'll come back later.'

'Don't be silly,' said Thembi with a smile. 'Where are you off to? You've only just arrived. Come here and meet my parents.' She looked at them then turned her head towards the boy. 'This is my friend Keith,' she said, and held out her hand for him to come closer. 'What did you want me to look at?'

Thembi's parents looked at each other and a message of hope flashed between them.

Keith's face was split by a wide grin and he was pointing to his legs. 'I got it, Thembi, I got it,' he shouted joyfully.

'Oh how wonderful!' she cried, as excited as he was.

Thembi explained briefly about his leg. Dikeledi secretly wiped a tear from her eye, and Maliyeza cleared his throat noisily.

Keith was dressed in a lightweight beige and green check woollen shirt and a pair of dark brown cords. On his feet were a pair of brown leather shoes and brown socks.

'Keith, you look super all dressed up like that,' said Thembi warmly. Her voice was very gentle when she spoke again. 'Does it hurt?'

'It doesn't *hurt* actually, but it does feel a bit peculiar. I took a few steps yesterday and walked for quite a long time this morning. I had to use crutches of course, and I got very tired, but everyone says I will only need them for a little while,' he said with pride. 'Of course, as I grow bigger I will have to get new legs made,' he added importantly.

He started to wheel himself away from the bed.

'I'd better be going now. I'll see you later,' he said with obvious reluctance.

'Have you got someone coming to see you?' asked Thembi.

'No. My Dad can't come during the day.'

'Then why don't you stay here with us?' said Thembi.

'Can I really?' he asked eagerly, his face lighting up.

'Of course you can. We want you to.'

The conversation became general and soon they were all laughing unrestrainedly as Keith told them about the times when his curiosity had landed him in hot water with the nursing staff. 'Should I go and ask Sister Dlamini to bring Mandy here?' asked Keith. 'She only gets visitors at night so she'll be in her cot all by herself now.'

'If you think Sister Dlamini will allow it, of course.'

Keith went off, and in a remarkably short time he returned, accompanied by the sister and Mandy.

'I'll leave Mandy here for a while if you like,' said the sister. 'Now you behave yourself, Mandy, and don't crawl all over Thembi's bed. I don't want you to hurt her legs. Understand?'

Wide blue eyes stared solemnly back at her as Mandy nodded her head.

They sat chatting for a while and after her parents had left, both feeling much happier about Thembi since seeing her with the children, Keith and Mandy stayed there until Sister Dlamini came to take Mandy back to her cot. She was very satisfied with the emotional progress Thembi appeared to be making.

Mduduzi walked into the ward that evening and stopped abruptly, the smile on his face fading. Thembi was propped up in bed, her hair brushed softly around her face. Her eyes shone and her face did not look nearly as thin as it had been.

She was laughing, and she held the hand of the red-headed boy seated beside her in a wheel-chair. Next to him was a man with an identical thatch of red hair, a look of love lighting his face as he watched his son talking away, the fingers of his free hand stabbing the air like punctuation marks.

Thembi, sensing his presence, glanced up and saw her fiancé. 'Mduduzi,' she cried delightedly, her face lighting up.

Ashamed of the fierce stab of jealousy which had ripped through him at the sight of her so happy with these strangers, he crossed quickly to her side and gathered her into his arms, hugging her tightly. His kiss was gentle but prolonged, a lingering stamp of possession.

'You're looking much better, *mayi dali*,' he said.

'I'm feeling fine – as long as I don't try to move my legs.'

He stood close beside her, holding her hands in his, and Thembi introduced him to the other two.

Keith sat silently looking at him with an unblinking gaze. Mduduzi gazed back at him and suddenly Keith relaxed and smiled. He held out his hand and Mduduzi solemnly shook it.

Keith had been in such a hurry to bring his father to meet Thembi that he had not had a chance to tell him about the new leg, so Mduduzi was invited to join in the first inspection. They were astounded at the flexibility of the joints and were loud in their admiration and strong in their encouragement. Keith and his father left soon afterwards and Mduduzi sat down on the side of Thembi's bed, taking her hands in his and holding them tightly.

'Am I hurting you?' he asked anxiously.

Thembi shook her head, smiling contentedly at him.

'Sorry to interrupt,' said a voice from the door and Sister Dlamini walked into the ward with Mandy in her arms.

'Mandy wants to kiss Duzi g'night,' stated the little girl, looking angelic in her warm, fluffy blue dressing gown, her blonde curls tumbling about her head.

Mduduzi had straightened up and was standing beside Thembi as the sister put Mandy down on the bed. Mandy caught sight of the teddy and squealed with delight as she pounced on it, holding it close and wriggling her way into Thembi's arms until she lay contentedly against her breast.

'Her therapy today was very strenuous and I think she is over-tired. Her parents had to leave early and we haven't been able to get her to settle. As she kept asking for Duzi I thought if she saw him it might help to calm her down. You don't mind, do you?' asked the sister.

'Of course not,' replied Thembi. 'She looks so peaceful lying here, doesn't she?' she added. 'In fact, she looks half asleep already.'

'I think you're right. Come, my little one. It's time for bed now. Thanks, Thembi, you've been a great help.' As she spoke, she took the teddy bear gently from Mandy, laid it down on the bed then tenderly lifted her into her arms. 'Say goodnight to everyone now.'

A sleepy smile was all they got as Mandy was taken back to her cot.

Thembi looked at Mduduzi in the silence which followed their departure.

He had resumed his position on the side of the bed and his features were sharply etched, as if drawn in pain, his eyes silently adoring her. When he spoke his voice was rough with emotion and it was evident that he was deeply moved.

'I don't think I have ever seen anything more beautiful

than you with that baby curled up against you,' he said. His voice was low and very intense.

He placed his hands on her pillow, one on either side of her head, and bent forward until his forehead rested on hers.

'Dear God, I love you. Each day you become more precious to me. Oh *sithandwa*, I need you so much. I merely exist between the times I can be with you. Nothing else has much meaning,' he said distractedly. 'When you fell ill I thought I was going to lose you and I nearly went out of my mind with worry. I pray that I never ever have to go through anything like that again.' His voice broke on the last words and he buried his face in the curve of her neck, seeking the strength and warmth which he desperately needed. Thembi lifted her arms and held him to her, her fingers gently stroking his neck.

Gradually a sense of peace stole over him and he was able to get a grip on his emotions before lifting his head to look down at her.

Cupping her face in the palms of his hands he moved his lips gently over hers then deepened the caress to a melting sweetness which could not disguise his passionate longing. Thembi's response was equally passionate, but her trembling mouth revealed her feelings. She loved and longed for him, but had fears and doubts about their future.

'I love you, Mduduzi, more than I can ever hope to tell you,' she whispered.

He raised his head and looked down at her. She lifted a hand and ran her fingers gently down his cheek before resting them on his lips.

He caught her hand and taking her fingers into his mouth, one by one, he slowly caressed the sensitive pads with the tip of his tongue, his eyes never leaving her face.

'Oh God, how I wish I didn't have to walk out of here without you,' he said raggedly, standing up in response to the end-of-visiting bell.

The next day two special things happened. The first was the arrival of a package soon after breakfast. In it was a teddy bear with a brief message: *For Mandy with our love*, signed by Mduduzi.

The second, and most incredible, was that she moved the toes of her left foot.

She was lying on her back on the therapy table. Jean was standing next to her with her fingers curled around the foot and she was laughing as she told Thembi a story about her younger son when she felt a flutter of movement beneath her hand.

She stopped talking in mid-sentence and not a muscle in her body moved. Every part of her was concentrated on her hand.

'Do that again,' she said quietly.

Again there was a faint movement.

She relaxed and turned to Thembi, her eyes bright with excitement, her face radiant.

'At last we've got a breakthrough!' she cried exultantly. 'We've done it!' Tears came unbidden into Jean's eyes as she removed her hand from Thembi's foot and wrapped her arms around her body, hugging her.

Thembi was too choked-up to speak and tears rolled down her cheeks, but there was a weak smile of achievement on her face.

'Thank God we've made a start. You realise, of course, that our work is only just beginning,' said Jean briskly. 'But oh lord, what a wonderful moment this is,' she added, a huge grin of pure delight spreading over her features.

Thembi's parents and Mduduzi were overcome with joy and gratitude and they looked forward to the time when she would recover fully from her illness. The hopelessness and helplessness of the past months were over.

7

Heart-break

For the next three months Thembi's life seemed to revolve around the therapy room and the swimming pool. Jean worked her till they were both fit to drop. By the time she was taken back to her bed each day Thembi felt as if she had been put through a mangle. But the results were worth every ounce of effort, every tear, every aching muscle.

Her left foot was getting stronger every day and they achieved success with the right one as well, although it was much slower to respond to treatment and much weaker than the left one.

Mandy and Keith had both gone home and although Thembi was friendly with the other people she met, she missed them very much.

A few of the friends she and Nomalizo had made at the ice rink came to see her one afternoon but the atmosphere soon became strained and uncomfortable, as everyone avoided the subject of skating. Apart from the ice rink, they had little in common. They did not come to visit her again.

A few of her friends from work came in to see her but they, too, found it an effort to keep conversation going. Thembi had lost touch with the outside world and what happened in the home was of little interest to the others.

As her physical condition improved so her emotional one deteriorated and no matter how much they tried, Mduduzi and her family were finding it more and more difficult to reach her.

Thembi was withdrawing into herself and although she smiled and laughed when they were with her, her eyes were sad.

She was building an invisible wall slowly around herself and even Mduduzi could not get through it.

She had been in the convalescent home for five months when Mr Carlstein announced it was time to get her on her feet. They were in the therapy room and he had been watching Jean and Thembi working together.

'Well, young lady, it won't be long before we get you mobile now. We are all very pleased with your progress,' he said.

Thembi was elated and at the same time terrified. It was so long since she had stood on her legs she feared their ability to support her.

'I'll arrange for the chap who does our orthopaedic work to come and measure you for boots and ankle supports and to organise crutches for you,' the doctor continued, a satisfied smile on his face.

'Boots! *Boots*? I am to wear *boots*?' Thembi burst out, horror-struck. A blank silence met her outburst.

'Just how did you imagine you would be able to start walking on those weakened ankles of yours without support for them?' asked the doctor kindly.

'I hadn't thought about it,' she whispered, a pinched look on her face.

He sat down opposite her and took her hands in his. When he spoke again his voice was soft and soothing, as if she was a frightened child needing reassurance.

'Your progress has been remarkable and you are a very lucky young woman,' he said. 'I told you in the beginning that you would probably be left with a weakness, but there is no reason to believe that you will have to wear boots for the rest of your life. In time you will be able to wear shoes again.'

Thembi thought sorrowfully of the rows of stylish shoes in the cupboard at home, shoes she would probably never be able to wear again. For the first time since she had become ill she realised that her life would have to change. She sat for a long time taking a good, long look at herself and her future before reaching a decision.

When Mduduzi walked into the ward that evening he sensed immediately that all was not well. Thembi was sitting up, her fingers nervously plucking at the counterpane, her head bent, her eyes downcast.

Sensing his presence she lifted his eyes and he caught his breath at the look of abject misery he saw there. He was beside her in moments.

'What is it, Thembi? For God's sake, tell me, what happened?' His voice trembled slightly with fear, a sense of grim foreboding filling him as she sat mutely looking at him, her eyes dull and agonized.

'Hello, Mduduzi,' she said at last, her voice low and not quite steady, her eyes once again downcast. 'I've been sitting here for the past hour wondering how to say this. It isn't easy and I don't want to hurt you.' She paused, as if gathering her courage before speaking again. 'Please forgive me, but I've realised that everything has changed. I've changed. I can't marry you,' she said, the last few words coming out in a rush, her voice so soft the words were barely audible.

Mduduzi closed his eyes for a few seconds, taking a couple of deep breaths as he tried to get a grip on himself. He sat down on the side of her bed, taking her restless fingers into his hands. They were cold and shaking.

'Why? What's happened to make you change your mind? Why are you doing this to us? Haven't we been through enough already?' His voice held bewilderment, pain, shock, as one question followed immediately on the other, without waiting for replies.

She raised her eyes to his face and closed them quickly at the sight of his features, his lips drawn into a taut grimace, his eyes pleading for an explanation.

When she opened her eyes again and looked at him, she had herself under rigid control.

'I've come to realise that I would be a dreadful burden to you if we were to marry. No, please, let me finish,' she said, swiftly placing the fingers of one hand over his lips as he opened them to speak. 'It is going to be a long time before I've recovered sufficiently to be independent. I'll be able to get about on crutches, admittedly, but what kind of life will it be for you? In your line of business it is essential that you mix socially and entertain and, believe me, I would be an embarrassment to you,' she said sadly.

'Stop it!' he said violently. 'That's nonsense and you know it. You could *never* be an embarrassment to me.'

'Oh yes, I would,' she contradicted him forcefully. 'I have watched the people who come to visit here. I have experienced it with people who are friends of mine, when they have come to see me. I have found that they look anywhere but at a handicapped person and worse still, there is nothing natural in their conversation. Every word is chosen with great care. You'd think that because a person has difficulty in walking that they've suddenly become dim-witted as well,' she said, her lips curling scornfully. 'Your friends would pity you and it wouldn't be long before you started to feel uncomfortable with them. I know what I'm talking about. I've seen it happen here.'

'Then, if that is the case, all my so-called "friends" can go to hell for all I care!' he replied vehemently.

'No, Mduduzi. You can't cut yourself off from other people because of me. I won't allow it. And what about us? You and I both want children and I don't know how long it would be before my legs could stand the strain of a pregnancy – if ever. I want your life to be happy and fulfilled. You deserve it. You're a wonderful person and I love you too much to see what we have being destroyed through frustration and bitterness.'

'So you'd rather destroy it now? You say you want me to be happy yet you're taking away the only thing in the world that would bring me happiness.'

'Don't, please. You'd be constantly worrying about me, wondering whether I was managing all right, whether I'd fallen and hurt myself. You'd probably be on the phone half a dozen times a day checking up, just to put your mind at rest. Your business would suffer. Then you'd come home at night to a wife who was utterly exhausted because I will still have to come back here three times a week for therapy and I will still have to do daily exercises. After that I'll be fit for absolutely nothing but bed. So instead of you coming home to a wife eager to soothe away the stress of your day and a dinner specially prepared for you, you will come home and have to play nursemaid. No, Mduduzi, I'm not prepared to put you through that.'

'I notice that you haven't asked how I feel or let me discuss this! Oh no, instead you've taken it upon yourself to decide what is best for me. I think you're being childish, seeing difficulties where they don't exist,' he bit out savagely.

'Can't you see? It's started already,' she said, a note of anguish in her voice. 'You've no idea what I'm talking about. You have never seen me when I'm brought back to the ward each day. From the time we first met you kept telling me you found me perfect. Well, I am no longer perfect. Please, Mduduzi, try to understand!' she begged, crying bitterly.

'No, I don't understand,' he said furiously. 'And for God's sake, stop crying! I'm waiting for you to explain yourself more clearly because, God help me, I'm too stupid to work out for myself how anyone can pretend to love another the way you say you love me and yet suddenly decide to throw it all away.'

Thembi gulped and silently looked at him with large, tear-filled eyes which were starting to reflect fear as he went on speaking, his eyes half closed, a frown on his forehead.

'*How dare you* presume to know how I feel or what I'd do? You obviously haven't the faintest idea of what makes me tick. You think my love for you is the fair-weather kind. I wonder just how deep your *supposed* love is for me.'

She flinched under his furious onslaught but remained silent. He lifted a hand to rake it through his hair and she cowered back.

'All right, I'll go,' he said, shoulders slumping in defeat. 'I can't pretend even to begin to understand what has brought all this about, but it is obvious that you've made up your mind and my presence is no longer welcome.' Standing up he looked down at her, his hands clenching and unclenching at his sides, his nostrils flaring, his face contorted.

'Damn you to hell, Thembi Gumbi,' he shouted, 'and I hope you'll be happy wallowing in your self-pity and misery!' He turned and stormed out of the ward, slamming the door violently behind him.

The realisation that he had walked out of her life forever galvanised Thembi into action. 'No, Mduduzi, please don't go – not like this!' she cried out, throwing back the bedclothes and swinging her legs over the side of the bed, instinctively intending to go after him. A shaft of pain like a red-hot blade sliced through her flesh and shot up one leg and into her thigh, causing her to cry out and bringing her to her senses and an awareness of what she was doing.

Blinded by tears, she tried to move to ease the pain and promptly lost her balance. The next thing she knew she was tumbling out of the bed, landing with a loud thump on the floor where she lay, momentarily winded, as pain ripped through her, causing her to cry out in anguish. Raising her voice, she shouted for help.

The door burst open and Sister Dlamini stood there nonplussed, taking in the scene as Thembi lay awkwardly, partly on her side and partly on her stomach, with one arm bent and her forehead resting on her forearm, while the other hand, tightly clenched into a fist, was hammering on the floor as she sobbed uncontrollably.

The sister rushed towards her, knelt down and slowly and carefully turned her patient over so that she could see her face.

'I saw Mr Mkhize go out with a face like a thunder cloud and I came to see whether you were all right,' she said. 'What happened?' she asked, gently supporting Thembi in her arms.

'If this is living, then I wish I was dead . . . *dead* . . . *DEAD*!' screamed Thembi, hitting out wildly with her still clenched fist, her voice rising until she was shrieking like a demented creature. The high-pitched keening sound was cut off abruptly as the sister slapped her sharply on the cheek. Thembi burst into tears, sobbing as if her heart would break, and Sister Dlamini turned her into her arms, cradling her head against her shoulder, pushing a handkerchief into her hand.

'Hush, love, hush. It's all over now,' she crooned softly running her hand over Thembi's head, gently massaging it. She went on, 'I'm sorry I had to hit you, love, but it was necessary. You understand, don't you?' Thembi nodded her head. 'Did you hurt yourself?' Again Thembi nodded her head, looking at the sister with swollen, red-rimmed eyes, her mouth trembling, sniffing now and then.

'I want you to stay just where you are. Don't move. I'm going to find someone to help me get you back into bed, then we'll take it from there. OK?' Thembi acknowledged the instruction and Sister Dlamini gently lowered her to the floor before standing up and hurrying from the ward. She was back almost immediately with three nurses and together they helped Thembi back into bed, settling her comfortably.

'Now then, tell me what happened,' said the sister when they were once again alone. Taking Thembi's hands into hers she looked keenly at her, waiting for the reply.

'I sat up and dangled my legs over the side of the bed and I lost my balance,' said Thembi, her head lowered, not looking up from their entwined hands as she replied.

'Where did you hurt yourself?'

'I got a terrible pain in my leg while I was sitting on the bed and then I think I banged myself on the arm of the chair as I fell.'

'Well, I'm going to give you something for the pain now. Mr Carlstein will be here presently to see you and I want you to lie quietly until he arrives. We had to phone to let him know what had happened and he says he'll call in to check if everything is OK.'

Thembi gripped the sister's hands as she gazed imploringly at her. 'Please don't tell my parents about this. They'll worry for nothing.'

❤

Mduduzi sat in his car fighting to ease the tension which held him in its grip. When he felt he had himself sufficiently under control he turned the ignition key and drove home, bewildered and frustrated. He could not believe that everything that made living worthwhile had suddenly been snatched from him.

When he reached home he got a bottle of whisky and a glass, and drank, then kept refilling the glass until he finally passed out, finding the unconsciousness he was looking for. The next morning he woke up with the worst hangover he had ever known.

He swallowed some aspirin tablets and made himself a large mug of strong, black coffee before sitting down and closing his eyes as he rested his head on the back of the chair in the lounge. Mingled with the pounding ache in his head were images of Thembi as she had looked the night before. He had known immediately he saw her that something was wrong. He remembered every word they had exchanged and the memory was like acid eating into his soul.

Coming to a sudden decision, he went to the telephone and dialled the hospital where Nomalizo worked.

'Can I see you, please?' he asked. 'I must speak to you.'

'It's about Thembi, isn't it?' she asked softly. 'Has she broken off the engagement?'

'Yes. But how the hell did you know so soon? It only happened last night!'

'I didn't know, but I've been expecting it for quite a while. Look, I can't speak now. We are terribly busy but I'll be off duty at four o'clock this afternoon. Meet me here.'

It was a good thing it was Sunday, thought Mduduzi, because he was not in any condition to go to work. He stared morosely at the ceiling as thoughts churned through his mind. He would speak to Nomalizo first then go and see Maliyeza and Dikeledi, he decided.

He lay there remembering everything that had happened since he and Thembi had met and the thought of living the rest of his life without her terrified him. There was nothing to look forward to but blank emptiness and dark despair. And he had waited so long for her to come into his life. He was still thinking of her when he drifted off to sleep. He awoke feeling much better, just in time to go to meet Nomalizo.

They did not raise the subject which was uppermost in both their minds until they were seated and had been served in a small restaurant not far from the hospital.

'OK, what happened?' she asked bluntly.

Mduduzi told her everything that had happened the evening before. After a few moments of silence she looked at him understandingly.

'I knew it was coming. The signs have been there for quite a while. The only thing is I am surprised it did not happen sooner,' said Nomalizo.

72

'What do you mean you knew it was coming? Did she say something to you?'

'No, but I don't think you realise just what she has been through these past six months. The pain you saw on the morning she went into hospital was a drop in the ocean compared to what she has suffered and will continue to suffer until the muscles in her legs have recovered and those awful exercises can be stopped. Of course, the healing process will speed up now that she is on her feet and ready to start walking again.

'By the time you visited her in the evenings she had had a few hours' sleep and she made sure that she was comfortable in bed and didn't have to move her legs. In that way she was able to put on a cheerful face and because of this, she has not allowed you or any of us to know a fraction of the agony she has had to endure. She wouldn't allow it because she won't permit herself to become an object of pity. No disabled person will.'

All the time she spoke, Nomalizo looked directly into his eyes. She saw that she had shocked him and she saw, too, the dawning understanding of the extent of Thembi's suffering, of which he and her parents had not been told.

'Oh my God,' he moaned, a look of desolation on his face. 'I didn't understand and I accused her of being childish. I must go to her. They must let me see her, even though it's past visiting time,' he said in desperation, putting down his serviette, preparing to leave.

'No!' said Nomalizo sharply, putting out a hand to stop him. 'You're not to go near her. Not at the moment, anyway. This is something she has to work out for herself. Believe me, Mduduzi, every patient I have seen like this has reacted in very much the same way as she has.' Her voice was soft and sympathetic. 'That's what I meant when I said I was surprised she waited so long. Something must have happened or been said yesterday which suddenly increased her feeling of insecurity and prompted her decision.

'I am going to phone Mr Carlstein and ask his permission to see her alone. I'll tell him what's happened and I'm sure he'll allow it, and as I know Jean Grant very well I'm also going to tell her. I can't pretend to know your feelings but my advice is to leave her alone until she comes to terms with herself,' she said.

'Thanks, Nomalizo. I needed your guidance. At the moment my future is blank. Up to now I've resented the limited time I've been allowed to see her but those few crumbs now seem like a feast compared to nothing at all. Have you finished your coffee?' he asked, changing the subject. 'For the first time in my life I deliberately drank myself into a stupor last night and I'm still feeling dreadful. I'd like to get out of here and into the fresh air.' They stood up and walked towards the door. 'Thanks for meeting me. You've helped tremendously and I think I'm beginning to see her point of view. I don't agree with it and it isn't going to be easy to accept, but at least I'm starting to understand.'

He drove Nomalizo back to the hospital and headed towards Thembi's home to discuss what had happened, grateful that her parents were there to turn to. He found himself leaning heavily on their strength and support.

They were sitting in the lounge after dinner. Dikeledi was knitting. Mduduzi was smoking, idly watching the smoke wreathe and curl before disintegrating into the air. Maliyeza was also smoking, a thoughtful expression on his face. He looked at the younger man as though weighing his words carefully before deciding to speak.

'How much work have you on hand at the moment, Mduduzi?' he asked. 'And how urgent is it?'

Mduduzi turned his attention to the older man. 'Not much,' he replied. 'I've been so worried about Thembi that I haven't taken on nearly as much as I normally would have done. The projects that are at present on the go can easily be handled by my staff. Why?'

'I was wondering if it might not be a good idea for you to get away for a while. Why not go to your parents for a month or so?' suggested Maliyeza. 'If Nomalizo is right, and I think she is, then Thembi needs to sort this problem out in her own way. It would probably be best for both of you to put some distance between you for the time being.'

Looking down at his hands Mduduzi carefully ground out his cigarette in the ashtray on the small table next to him before once again raising his eyes.

'I don't know. I really don't know where to go from here,' he sighed. 'All those months of tension and worry, and now this! At the moment I feel completely lost and I know I won't be able to settle to any work until I can accept this. I feel devastated. I can't think of any other word to describe my reaction. Maybe a break *is* the answer. I don't know. What I *do* know is that I can't face being alone in my apartment because, although she has only been there once, Thembi's presence is everywhere.' His voice broke and he put his head into his hands, his elbows resting on his knees.

Dikeledi stood up and went to him. She stroked her hand over his head as she would a child, in an effort to show her sympathy and understanding.

'I think Maliyeza is right, you know. You are going to make yourself ill if you carry on like this. You have lost weight in the past few weeks as it is, and there are lines of strain on your face which shouldn't be there,' she said.

He looked up at her and took her hand into both of his, drawing comfort and reassurance from her.

'There is nothing we would like more than to see you and Thembi together, but we must think of her as well and remember that she, too, must be suffering now as a result of her decision. It couldn't have been easy for her,' continued Dikeledi. 'Go to your parents. Spend time with them. Rest.

Take long walks along the beach. Give yourself a chance to think and please remember, we are always here if you need us.'

He squeezed her hand to show his gratitude and affection, then coming to a sudden decision, he stood up and prepared to leave.

'I think you are right. I *will* go to Cape Town. I'll keep in touch. I hope you know how much I appreciate your support.'

8

The Concert

For Thembi the days that followed were bleak. She had no interest in anything. One morning, after two completely unproductive hours in the therapy room, Jean stopped what they were doing and looked down at Thembi.

'You are going to have to snap out of this depression and self-pity, my girl,' she said sternly. Her voice was filled with rebuke and she hardened her heart to the shocked and hurt expression on Thembi's face. 'You were making such wonderful progress. And now look at you! As far as I'm concerned, we're wasting our time and either you put your mind to the work we have to do or I am afraid I am going to ask someone else to take over.' Jean hoped her words would get a positive reaction from Thembi. They did.

'I'm sorry, I really am,' said Thembi remorsefully. 'I have been a misery and you are right – I have to get on with living, even if it isn't what I would have chosen. I promise I will give you all I've got from now on.'

She was as good as her word. Within two weeks she was on her feet and once she had mastered the art of using crutches, her progress was swift and steady. A week later she went home.

Nobody mentioned Mduduzi and Thembi smothered the urge to ask if they had heard from him. She'd made her decision and she must live with it and allow time to heal the wound of their parting.

Dikeledi took her to the convalescent home on the days she had to go for therapy and she supervised Thembi's daily exercises. She was as strict as Jean had been and their efforts were amply rewarded by the slow evidence of the strengthening of the wasted muscles and less pain.

Thembi looked much better, though her ankles were weak and she tired very easily. Apart from the fact that she had to wear the hated boots and supports and use crutches, it was difficult to believe that she had ever been ill.

During one of her treatments Jean told her about a variety show that was being arranged to raise funds to build a clubhouse where the disabled could gather socially.

'There is a great need for a place like this. I am the treasurer of the fund-raising committee,' she said. 'We are hoping to raise enough money not only to build but to equip the place with a tv, a small library, a music centre and a variety of games. Nomalizo has told me how well you sing and play the piano. How about helping us with the show?'

'You mean you want me to get up on a stage as I am? On crutches?' Thembi asked, biting her lower lip, obviously very disturbed by the idea.

'No. Not on crutches. I thought it would make a greater impact if you used a wheel-chair,' replied the older woman with a sly grin. 'Your Editor is arranging publication of a story about the centre a week before we have the show and he is going to get some copies of the article printed which we will give out as handbills to the audience as they come into the hall. Come on, Thembi. A couple of the other performers will also be disabled. It will be far more comfortable for you than standing there leaning on crutches.'

'OK,' said Thembi at last, shrugging her shoulders. 'Why not?'

'Wonderful,' replied Jean, visibly relaxing. 'I'll arrange for Peter Masters to get in touch with you. He's in charge of this and he's also the leader of the band that will be playing in the show.'

Peter was energetic and enthusiastic about the show and was delighted with Thembi's musical talent.

He and the band had come to her home for a rehearsal one evening soon after they had met and before they left they were invited to use the Gumbi home for all their rehearsals. It wasn't long before Thembi, her mother, and Maliyeza too, found themselves totally committed to helping with the production and organisation as well of the show. The weeks that followed were happy ones for Thembi.

Her days were filled with activity which included her regular exercise. It was only in bed at night that she still mourned the loss of Mduduzi. It was like a dull ache which would not ease, no matter how much she assured herself she had made the right decision. Every day was proof of how dependent she was on her mother. She was useless without crutches to enable her to get around. She tired easily and often needed to lie down and rest. She was convinced that her decision had been the right one.

On the day of the show Dikeledi insisted that Thembi rest for most of the day. They all knew that it was going to take courage for her to face a large audience while she was singing and playing the piano. Tonight would be a challenge and no doubt an ordeal for her.

Thembi dressed carefully for the show. The full skirt of her gown fell in deep folds about her legs while the bodice clung lovingly to her slender waist and gentle curves. The shimmering of the mother-of-pearl fabric reflected the light, appearing to have a life of its own with each movement she made, highlighting her creamy dark complexion. A strand of pearls and matching ear studs were her only jewellery. She was no longer simply attractive, she was now positively beautiful, with an indefinable quality of self-confidence, compassion and strength which had not been evident before her illness.

As Thembi finished brushing her hair, Dikeledi came into the room with a broad smile on her face, her hands behind her back.

'All ready?' she asked.

'Just about. Oh Mama, I'm so nervous,' she said apprehensively.

'There is no need to be nervous. You are going to be just fine. You can come in, Maliyeza, she's decent,' called Dikeledi, looking over her shoulder to her husband who was waiting in the passage.

'Thembi, you look superb,' he said, stooping to kiss her cheek.

'Thanks, Baba. I'm scared out of my wits.'

'Nonsense. I've never known you to be scared of singing. Your mother and I have brought you a gift. We hope you like it.'

As Thembi looked inquiringly at them, Dikeledi brought her hands from behind her back. Dangling from the index finger of each one was a white boot.

Thembi looked stunned for a moment and then her face lit up with delight and excitement, her eyes shimmering with unshed tears at the thoughtfulness of these two people whom she loved with all her heart.

'Oh Mama, Baba,' she whispered. 'They're beautiful – for boots, that is,' she said shakily as she took them from her mother and swiftly bent and removed the hated black ones from her feet, replacing them with the white.

'You know, Thembi, with that long skirt leaving only the toes of your feet showing, nobody is going to know that you're not wearing shoes,' said Dikeledi. 'As a matter of fact, they'll probably think you're a fraud. I've never seen anyone look healthier than you do tonight.'

'Thank you both, not only for these, but for everything you've done for me, for your encouragement and support during the past months and for helping with the show. I have the most wonderful parents in the world and I love you both very dearly,' said Thembi with deep sincerity.

Dikeledi wiped the tears from her eyes and Maliyeza blew his nose vigorously to hide his emotion.

'Thank you, *mayi dali*, and you don't have to be told how much we love you. And now I think it's time we were leaving,' said her mother.

When they arrived at the hall Thembi insisted on walking in. Maliyeza brought her wheel-chair from the car and the family went inside.

The City Hall had been hired at a reduced rate for the function because it seated the most people and arrangements had secretly been made for the Council nursery to supply and install large tubs of growing palm trees and potted flowering shrubs.

'Oh Lord, isn't this beautiful? It's like walking into a garden,' breathed Dikeledi in awed amazement as they walked into the hall.

Thembi had been watching where she placed her crutches as she walked, so had missed the first impact of the décor. When she stood still and lifted her head she was speechless, her eyes enormous with surprise. The hall had been transformed into a paradise.

There were quite a few of the performers backstage and Thembi soon found herself caught up in the excitement of the final preparations before the show began. Tension was high and nerves were stretched to breaking point until the time came for the compère to go out front and get the show going. After that, the time seemed to fly as one performer after another went on stage and each one was enthusiastically applauded.

Thembi had been chosen to appear just before the interval and again to close the show. While the compère was introducing her to the audience and telling them of her background, as he had done with all the performers, Thembi was busy seating herself at the piano. When she was settled the spotlight was focused on her and she smiled serenely at the audience before pulling the microphone standing next to the piano closer to her.

'Good evening, everyone,' she said. 'We are going to play a medley of songs and we want you all to join in singing with us. If you don't know the words, then hum the tune or just clap your hands, but we want you all to join in. Here we go, then.' Her voice had been husky when she started speaking but she soon lost her nervousness as she concentrated on what she was saying and then on her hands as she and the band started to play the first of two numbers which were currently at the top of the hit parade. Voices were soon joining hers, coming from all parts of the hall. The next two songs were from the seventies and more and more people started to sing as they recognised the tunes and it was evident from their enthusiasm that they were thoroughly enjoying themselves.

Then the band swung into 'Mama Thembu's Wedding' from *Ipi Tombi*, followed by a favourite of the Zulu people, *'Iqhida Lendlela'*. The hall was soon filled with the sound of raised voices, hands clapping and feet stamping in time to the music.

As the last song came to an end the applause was tumultuous. There was no way that the audience were going to let Thembi go. After three more numbers they reluctantly let her go and the curtain was lowered.

Thembi sat quietly in the dressing room during the interval. She realised she was shaking and needed time to gather herself and prepare mentally for her second appearance. Sitting at the piano and being part of the band, she had not felt conspicuous but she knew the finale was going to be a vastly different story.

While the second half of the programme was on she went and sat quietly in the wings and watched as one act followed another, drawing strength and encouragement from these new friends who were giving their best.

She heard the compère introducing her again and she wheeled herself slowly on to the stage and over to where he stood waiting for her. She smiled at him and took the microphone, then faced the hall and waited for the audience to settle down after their spontaneous burst of applause at her appearance.

The band played the introduction to her first number and when she sang the first note the adrenalin started pumping, all nervousness fell from her and she started to enjoy herself. She was lost in the words and music of 'Memory' and then, in response to the applause and enthusiastic calls for more, she sang 'Don't cry for me, Argentina'.

After the last note died away the audience went wild with applause and she sat quietly waiting until they realised that she was not yet finished and quietened down. When there was not a sound from them Thembi lifted the microphone and started to speak.

'Ladies and gentlemen, I have been asked by the organisers to express our very deep gratitude for the wonderful support you have given us tonight and I would like to tell you how this project came into being. There is an elderly Jewish gentleman in Johannesburg who was living in Germany during the war. He was a young man in his mid-teens when his home was raided one night by the Gestapo and his family were taken away and lost to him forever. He managed to escape in the confusion of the raid and after enduring much hardship he finally reached our country, where he has lived ever since.

'Every week he goes to the home where I have been. He knows us all by name. He knows all about our medical problems and our families. He is a very special person and very easy to talk to and pour your heart out to. He is very kind, with a marvellous sense of humour and we all love him dearly even though none of us knows his name. We all call him simply Uncle Joe.

'The idea of a haven was his and he has given us a plot of ground for this purpose. He has set up a trust fund to cover rates and maintenance but we have to find the money for the building. This show tonight is the first of our fund-raising efforts and we thank you all for your support and for being such a warm and wonderful audience.'

All the while she had been speaking there was not a sound from anyone. Suddenly the silence was broken by a small voice. 'Thembi, Mandy bringed Duzi,' it said.

There was a burst of laughter from those sitting nearby and the tension was broken.

Thembi raised her left hand to shield her eyes from the glare of the footlights and, as her vision adjusted, she saw Mandy sitting in the front row, her teddy bear clutched in her arms. Seated on one side of her was a woman Thembi took to be her mother and on the other side was Keith, dressed in a light blue suit, with a huge grin on his face.

Putting the microphone in her lap, Thembi raised her right hand and blew them a kiss. The audience loved it.

'Hello Mandy . . . Keith,' she said, the microphone once again in her hand. 'These are two very dear friends of mine who were in the home at the same time as I was,' she explained. 'They both brought a great deal of love into all our lives.'

A loud burst of clapping followed.

'And now we would like to close the show on a more serious note,' she continued, turning to Peter and nodding her head to show that she was ready. She had chosen an air from *Messiah*. The music filled the hall, the words bringing hope and comfort to all who heard them.

> Come unto Him all ye that labour,
> Come unto Him that are heavy laden
> And He will give you rest.
> Take His yoke upon you and learn of Him
> For He is meek and lowly of heart

And ye shall find rest,
And ye shall find rest unto your soul.

As the last pure, resonant note died away the silence was complete. It lasted for a full five seconds before the audience erupted with a frenzied, thunderous ovation.

Thembi bowed her head. Then Peter called the full cast on to the stage. As each one came into view they were met with a fresh round of cheering and clapping until everyone was on stage. Then the curtain was lowered for the last time and the house lights were turned on.

Thembi found that she had moved too near the footlights to be hidden by the descending curtain. As she turned to wheel herself away, her eyes ranged over the audience, some of them already leaving the hall.

As her brain registered the message relayed by her eyes, her hands froze on the wheels of the chair. At the end of the third row from the front was Mduduzi, waiting while the woman in the seat next to him gathered up her things, stood up and joined him. Placing an arm protectively about her shoulders he guided her into the aisle before walking with her towards the exit.

Although totally incapable of moving, Thembi found that her mind had faithfully recorded every detail of both Mduduzi and his companion. He looked as if he had lost weight and from the glimpse she'd had of his face, he looked more serious. His companion was beautiful, petite and delicate with perfectly groomed black hair cut close to her head.

Thembi was never able to recall how she got back to her dressing room. She felt as if she had been whipped, so intense was the pain.

Only two thoughts kept hammering in her mind. Mduduzi hadn't waited very long to replace her in his life. As she had broken their engagement what else could she expect?

She wished with all her heart that he had not come tonight

and that she had not seen him because the wound of her longing had been unexpectedly and viciously slashed wide open again.

Everyone clambered excitedly into the dressing room to share their joy. Thembi acknowledged the praise and congratulations with apparent enjoyment, a smile fixed on her face. No one looking at her could possibly have guessed that her pleasure over the success of the evening had completely gone. As soon as she could, she asked her parents to take her home, saying she was exhausted.

She did not mention having seen Mduduzi and they did not speak of him either. As soon as they reached home she thanked them for all their help then went straight to her room and got into bed.

However she could not sleep. She lay for a long time in the dark thinking of what might have been and silently cursing fate for the way her life had been so cruelly disrupted. Her dreams were wild and confused and she woke up weary and unrefreshed. But during the long, black night she had come to a decision.

9

Salvation

'But why do you want to go to Port Elizabeth?' asked Dikeledi.

'Because I want to get away for a while, Mama,' Thembi replied. 'I thought I'd ask Nomalizo if she can get some time off to go with me. We could stay in our holiday apartment.'

Dikeledi sighed and shrugged her shoulders. 'You always were stubborn and I suppose I'm behaving like an old hen with one chick, which is precisely what I am,' she said wryly. 'OK, see if Nomalizo wants to go with you and if she can get leave. Your father's not going to be too happy about you going, of that you can be sure.'

Nomalizo was delighted with the suggestion and arrangements were soon made. She had managed to get a month's leave and early on the Saturday morning following the concert the two girls strapped themselves into Nomalizo's car. Their luggage was stowed in the boot and on the back seat was a box of groceries and a couple of tins of home-made cookies and biscuits which Dikeledi had made for them. They waved goodbye to Thembi's parents as Nomalizo released the clutch and they were on their way.

Thembi hadn't been to the apartment for a while and she stood in the middle of the lounge looking around as memories of childhood holidays spent there washed over her. She had always loved it.

It was late in the afternoon before they took a ride through the town then drove along the esplanade, finally parking near the beachfront. They sat on one of the benches overlooking the deserted beach, enjoying the peace and remarking on the many changes that had taken place since they had last been in the city.

'Let's go and say hello to Mama Thoka and Baba Vusi,' said Thembi when they returned home. The girls were surprised to find that their friends had moved out of their apartment and bought a house in Fernlands, a very exclusive suburb some distance from the city. The house was set back from the road, effectively screened from view by tall shrubs and flowering trees. The view from the driveway of the harbour and the open sea was spectacular.

Thoka Ndlovu's greeting was warm and enthusiastic as she shepherded the girls indoors and led them through to the lounge. Like Dikeledi, Thoka was a very caring and vibrant person.

'We were so sorry to hear about your illness, Thembi,' she said. 'It must have been a very worrying time for everyone. Thank God you have recovered as well as you have.'

'Yes,' said Nomalizo. 'She has been extremely fortunate. Her specialist has assured us that eventually, apart from a weakness in her ankles, there should be no lasting handicap.'

'We were surprised to find that you had moved,' broke in Thembi, not wanting to prolong the discussion on her illness.

'We only moved about a month ago,' replied their hostess. 'I haven't even written to tell your mother yet. We love it here and I'm having a wonderful time in the garden, after all those years in the apartment,' she said, smiling broadly.

The rest of the day sped by with much talking and laughing and remembering the good times they had enjoyed together when the children were small.

'How are Mandla and Baba Vusi?' asked Thembi.

'They're well. They are in partnership now as Mandla decided to study architecture.'

Before they realised it the afternoon was fading into evening. Thembi was just about to say that it was time they started back home when the front door opened and a very big man stepped inside. He was well over six feet tall.

Heavily fringed lashes covering sparkling brown eyes

emphasised his strong and ruggedly masculine features, softened slightly by the sensuality of his mouth. He was clean shaven and well proportioned with not an ounce of superfluous flesh. He looked about thirty years old.

'Thembi!' he exclaimed delightedly, putting his briefcase down. He strode over to her chair and stretched out his arms to scoop her up in a bear hug, planting a kiss on her surprised mouth.

'It's good to see you again,' he said sincerely. 'It's been a long, long time since we last met, hasn't it, Mama?'

'*Sawubona*, Mandla,' replied Thembi, laughing a bit self-consciously. 'It's good to see you, too. Do you remember my cousin Nomalizo?'

'Very vaguely. She must have been very small when last we saw one another,' he said, putting Thembi back into her chair and turning to the other girl. 'Our school holidays never coincided and boarding school was a long way from home,' he added slowly, his eyes pinned on her face.

Lowering her eyes shyly Nomalizo strove to overcome the breathlessness she was feeling.

'I'm delighted to meet you again, Nomalizo,' said Mandla simply, holding her small hand in his large one, apparently quite content just to stand there and gaze at her.

'Haven't you got a soccer practice this evening, Mandla?' asked Thoka, breaking in on the now silent couple who stood looking intently at each other.

'Yes, I have,' replied her son, releasing Nomalizo's hand and shaking his head as if to clear it. 'Are you girls staying for dinner?' he asked eagerly.

'We've been here all day,' laughed Thembi in reply. 'I think we should be getting home now, don't you Nomalizo?'

'Yes, I think we should. You still have your therapy ahead of you and you must not over-tire yourself,' was the reply. She looked from Mandla to Thoka. 'We only arrived yesterday so we have plenty of time to take you up on your invitation if it stays open,' she added, with a hint of mischief in her smile.

'Of course it's open, any time you want it to be,' replied Thoka.

'You'll have to excuse me,' said Mandla, obviously reluctant to leave. 'If I don't move now I'll never get to that practice. I'll be in touch with you,' he said as he turned to go from the room. He looked at Nomalizo as he spoke.

Within three days the cousins were persuaded into spending the remainder of their holiday in the Ndlovu's home. With each succeeding day it became more obvious that Mandla and Nomalizo were strongly attracted to each other. Thembi's pleasure in her cousin's happiness was tinged with a trace of bitterness as she thought frequently of Mduduzi and the happiness they had so briefly shared then lost.

On the Saturday after arriving at the coast Mandla carried Thembi on to the beach where they all settled themselves in the shade of a large umbrella, lazily leaning back in deck chairs.

'I think we ought to go somewhere nice for dinner, don't you girls?' asked Mandla as they were on their way home.

'Thanks, but count me out. I'm exhausted,' said Thembi, her eyes closed, her head resting tiredly on the back of the seat. 'You and Nomalizo go and have a drink for me.'

'Oh Thembi, I can't go and leave you at home,' said Nomalizo with a worried frown on her face.

'Nonsense. Of course you can. I won't be alone, I'll be with the family. And in any case, what are you going to do after I'm asleep? I plan to go to bed very early tonight. The sea air has worn me out. It would be stupid for you not to go and enjoy yourselves,' she said firmly.

Thembi was glad she had insisted on staying at home when she saw them just before they left. They looked so right together and Nomalizo had never looked prettier. As they planned to go dancing after dinner, Nomalizo had chosen to wear a red taffeta dress which lent a vibrant glow to her sparkling eyes.

Mandla, in a white suit and deep blue shirt, looked splendid and the way he took Nomalizo's arm as they said goodnight was very touching, making a deep impression on those staying behind. It was impossible not to recognise the attraction that had sprung up between them.

Thembi settled down for a while with Thoka and Vusi, a very quiet man who was content to sit and talk or read or join the others if they wanted to watch tv. He looked forward each day to the peace of his home and wife after the stress and strain of the day's work.

The picture of Nomalizo and Mandla as they had walked out of the door together remained in Thembi's mind and she could not have been happier for them, but she was totally unable to control the envy and bitterness within herself and it frightened her. Was she to live the rest of her life envying others their happiness? To feel sorry for herself and frustrated, as if she was trapped in a world where there was no place for happiness such as she and Mduduzi had once shared?

As each day passed she felt more and more despondent and inadequate but she succeeded in hiding her feelings from the others.

Mandla hurried home each evening and usually took them for a drive before dinner. They drove through the different suburbs as well as the city centre and he showed them the buildings which he and his father had designed.

Thembi's favourite route was along the marine drive and she looked forward to the moments when they stopped on the crest of a hill with a clear view of the sea spread out beneath them. The rocky coastline was magnificent in its grandeur, standing solid while the white-tipped waves crashed relentlessly against the rocks in a repetitive action as old as time itself. She found it very soothing to watch the ebb and flow of the tide.

'You won't mind if I take Nomalizo dancing this evening, will you Thembi?' asked Mandla during dinner one evening. They had been with the Ndlovus for just over a week and Mandla had taken Nomalizo out alone twice during that time.

'Of course not,' she replied. 'You must make the most of the time we have left,' she said, smiling. 'I will probably watch the movie on tv. I was in hospital when it was released so I haven't seen it. You go and enjoy yourselves and don't worry about me.'

Later, as Thembi lay in the darkness, she felt ashamed of herself as she recalled her feelings when Nomalizo had walked into the lounge before she and Mandla had left. A fierce, devastatingly destructive feeling of bitter envy had caught her unawares as she had watched her cousin's glowing face and seen the momentary blaze of near-adoration in Mandla's eyes as he had looked down at her.

They had hardly left when Thembi said she had changed her mind about watching the movie, excused herself and went into her room. Unaware of the tears which slowly trickled down her cheeks, she lay there thinking of the things she would never again be able to do. Dance. Ice skate. Wear elegant shoes. Run along the beach at the water's edge. Be a part of Mduduzi's life. Her sleep was not a restful one.

'Mandla has asked some of his friends around tomorrow night,' said Thoka cheerfully a few days later. 'He's been wanting to do it for some time but he never seemed to get around to it. I think having you girls here has finally spurred him on to get going. You will help me with the preparations, won't you?'

The next evening a large group of young people gathered on the lawn and Thembi and Nomalizo were introduced to the other members of Mandla's soccer team and their partners. The evening could not have been more perfect. There was not a cloud in the sky nor any wind, and the air was warm with a faint salty tang from the sea.

There was music and a lot of laughter with good-humoured banter and teasing among the men. Mandla kept Nomalizo close beside him and Thembi stayed seated on a lounger, not too keen to walk around and be conspicuous on her crutches. Mandla and Nomalizo kept her glass filled and saw that she had all she wanted to eat. Although she appeared to be enjoying herself, Thembi wished that the evening was over and she could relax and be herself.

The evening had shown her more clearly than anything else that her decision regarding Mduduzi was the right one. She would have been a social disaster to him.

A couple of days after the party Mandla came home early and they were sitting in the lounge drinking tea.

'I saw Barbara Laing when I was out shopping this afternoon,' said Thoka. 'She told me that Debbie and John are getting married on Saturday,' she added, looking at her son.

He frowned, looking enquiringly at her. 'We haven't had an invitation to the wedding, have we? I never saw one.'

'No, there was no invitation. It is to be a private, family only affair.'

'Why private? And why so sudden? I saw them about three weeks ago and they didn't say anything about getting married. Debbie isn't pregnant, is she?' he asked.

'No, she isn't pregnant.' Thoka looked very sad. 'She's got leukaemia. The specialist estimates no more than six months before the end.'

'Holy God,' breathed Mandla appalled, his suddenly nerveless fingers sending his teacup crashing into its saucer, as the shock waves rippled through the room. 'Not Debbie!' he cried disbelievingly, staring at his mother, his mind grappling with this bombshell. 'John idolises that girl. He must be absolutely devastated!'

'I imagine that the whole family is devastated,' replied his mother sadly. Turning to the girls she explained that Barbara was Debbie's aunt and she had felt that as the boys had been friends since boarding school days John would like Mandla to know.

'Apparently as soon as they were told, John insisted on getting married and met with tremendous opposition from Debbie. But he has finally made her realise that he wants to share everything with her in the time they have left to them, the depths as well as the heights, as Barbara put it, and he refused point blank to take no for an answer to be shut out of her life now,' said Thoka.

'Oh, what a tragedy,' said Nomalizo with a catch in her voice. 'I certainly admire that young man. It won't be easy for either of them but I'm glad for her sake that he'll be with her.'

The silence which followed was oppressive, each one lost in their own thoughts.

Suddenly Mandla stood up. 'Come along, girls,' he said, his voice betraying his agitation. 'Let's go down to the beach for a while. I must get some of this agony out of me. I won't be long, I'm going to change into my track suit. And I suggest you girls do the same. I think it might rain.'

A short while later Thembi sat alone on a bench on the promenade, her gaze following the tiny figures of Nomalizo and Mandla in the distance as they jogged along the deserted beach.

She was enjoying the solitude as well as the glowing splendour of the setting sun, the dull roar of waves breaking on the shore and the occasional cry of a seagull.

Her thoughts turned to the unknown Debbie and John and her mind conjured up a picture of Mduduzi's face when she had told him she couldn't marry him. His bewilderment, his plea for understanding and finally, his anger. With blinding clarity she saw that he had been wanting to share her trouble and all that life held for her just as John wanted to share with Debbie. Without even trying to see his point of view, she had broken their engagement and ended their relationship. She had thought only of herself, even though she had fooled herself into believing it was best for him.

'Oh God, what have I done?' she cried silently. She hadn't been prepared to give them a chance to work things out, despite the fact that he had been there, solid, supportive and loving throughout the worst time of her illness. Hadn't he continually told and shown her how much he loved her? She had repaid him by wrapping her misery and self-pity around her like a cloak, not giving them a chance to tackle the problems.

As she sat there thinking about the courage Debbie would need, knowing what lay ahead of her, a thought flashed through Thembi's mind, as clearly as if the words had been written on a screen before her eyes. 'I complained because I had no shoes until I saw a man who had no feet'. She realised how foolish and thoughtless she had been. The doctor had repeatedly told her that she would eventually be able to lead a normal if slightly restricted life, whereas Debbie would have no chance to appreciate and enjoy to the full the gift of life at all beyond, possibly, six months.

Thembi began to shed tears, not harsh or destructive but gentle, cleansing, healing ones. When her tears had dried Thembi felt as if she had been washed clean of all the anger, frustration and bitterness that had been eating away at her and she knew that the time had come to put all that had happened behind her, to look forward with confidence to each day and be thankful for the blessings it brought. She still had a future to look forward to.

10

Wedding Bells

Later that evening, as they were having dinner, Thembi told them how her eyes had been opened and she did not spare herself when admitting how ashamed she felt about her recent selfishness.

'No, Thembi,' broke in Nomalizo hastily, stretching out her hand to clasp her cousin's fingers within her own. 'You have nothing whatsoever to feel ashamed about. Everyone in a situation such as yours has to come to terms with it in their own way and in their own time.'

'I know,' said Thembi, 'and believe me I now know how fortunate I am and how much worse off I could have been. Mama and Baba have been wonderful and I know my illness put a lot of strain on them. I realise I have wasted a lot of precious time but now feel I want to start really living again. I realise how much I have going for me. I know what I'll do first. I'll get my car converted so that I can start driving again. I know I can do it!'

Thembi's face was aglow with enthusiasm and excitement as she planned her immediate future and Nomalizo uttered a silent prayer of thanks for the transformation. The others watched and listened with joy in their hearts.

'When would you like to go home?' Nomalizo asked quietly. Not by a flicker of an eyelid did she show that she had no wish to leave Port Elizabeth sooner than they had planned.

Mandla was not so calm. 'What do you mean, when would she like to go home? You still have nine or ten days of your holiday left,' he said crossly. His parents turned to stare at him in amazement. His features were set in cold, harsh lines and for a moment there was not a trace of their normally placid, happy-go-lucky son.

Nomalizo did not look at anyone when she replied, her head bent down, her eyes studying the design on the plate in front of her, her hands resting on the tablecloth.

'Thembi has just told us she is ready to pick up the threads of her life. We have waited for months for her to come to grips with her problem. She is naturally impatient to start,' she said.

Thembi felt uncomfortable in the silence that followed but appreciated her cousin's understanding and support.

'Would you mind if we left on Saturday?' she asked tentatively, glancing at them all as she answered the question which had triggered off the tension at the table.

'Of course not. If that's what you want, then Saturday it is,' answered Nomalizo calmly, taking it upon herself to speak for them all. She raised her head and looked at Vusi and Thoka before continuing, 'We've had a wonderful holiday here and we've loved every moment but the time has come for it to end. Just now Thembi's welfare must come first. After all, that's why we came here in the first place, isn't it? I'm sure you will understand why we must cut short our stay.' As she finished speaking she looked pleadingly at Mandla before turning her attention once again to her dinner.

Thoka and Vusi expressed their disappointment at the sudden decision but made no attempt to get them to change their minds.

Mandla said nothing, staring morosely at the floral arrangement in the centre of the table.

After dinner Thembi phoned home. Full of self-confidence and sounding like her old self she told her mother that they would be leaving for home at the weekend.

Dikeledi called her husband to the phone, unable to believe the change in their daughter. After he had replaced the receiver he turned to his wife and wrapped his arms around her. 'Thank you, God,' was all he said.

Later that evening Mandla took Nomalizo by the hand and led her into the garden, guiding her away from the house and into a secluded corner.

They stood facing each other, silently looking into one another's eyes. Then with a muffled groan he reached out and drew her close, kissing her lingeringly and with devastating thoroughness, his hands moving restlessly up and down her back and over her hips, moulding her slender form closely to his. Nomalizo clasped him tightly around the waist then lifted one arm to encircle his neck as she pressed herself against him, returning his burning kisses with unexpected ardour.

'You can't go,' he said. 'Not yet. I can't lose you now that I've only just found you. I thought we'd have at least another ten days or so together and now it's suddenly dwindled down to no more than three. I love you, Nomalizo, and I want to marry you. I hadn't intended saying anything just yet because I was afraid you'd say it was too soon. But this sudden decision to go has changed things. Will you, my *sithandwa*? Will you marry me?' His voice was hoarse with tension.

She drew back and gazed at him, her eyes brilliant with love.

'Oh yes,' she breathed, her usual serenity completely shattered. 'Yes, please,' was her simple reply. She twined both arms around his neck and gave herself up to the wonder of his loving, returning it in full measure.

'Soon, *mayi dali*? How soon?'

'Just as soon as I have worked my notice and we can make all the arrangements,' she replied, her voice trembling exultantly. 'I love you so much that the thought of leaving you has been tearing me apart all evening, but I dared not let Thembi know,' she said, snuggling close, wanting to be a part of him, returning his overwhelmingly demanding kisses with feverish abandonment.

He drew back his head, resting his cheek on the crown of her head, his arms holding her close. 'I'm going with you on Saturday,' he announced.

'How can you?' she asked. 'What about your work?'

'As it's nearly time for the building industry to close for the Christmas holidays I have nothing urgent on hand. I'm sure my father won't mind if I go away for three or four days next week. I'll drive you home, meet your family and spend as much time as I can with my future wife,' he said smugly, relaxing now that he had found a way to delay their parting.

'Oh you clever darling, what a wonderful idea!' she exclaimed delightedly, squeezing him tightly in her enthusiasm. 'You can stay with us and we can sort out the details of the wedding while you're there. I will still be on leave next week so we can spend all the time together,' she went on.

'*All* the time together?' he teased, then hugged her to show how happy he was. 'I don't think my parents or Thembi are going to be surprised when they hear our news. I haven't exactly made a secret of the way I feel about you.'

The night was quiet, the air calm and the reflection of the moon cut a silver pathway across the surface of the sea. Reluctant to bring the wonder of their new-found happiness to an end they sat close together on a garden bench, her head resting on his shoulder, their arms about each other, gazing at the tranquil scene before them and talking softly far into the night.

———— ♥ ————

Thembi leaned forward, her weight on the palms of her hands which rested on the back of the bench where Mandla and Nomalizo had sat sharing their dreams two nights earlier, her crutches resting beside her.

She looked out at a scene similar to the one they had

watched, the only difference being that the moon had not yet risen and the sky still faintly flushed with the last lingering glow of the setting sun.

She felt a slight touch of regret at having to leave this peace and beauty behind, but it was quickly replaced by the joyous thought of going home.

The night before had been one she would always remember. Mandla and Nomalizo had broken their news at breakfast and everyone had been so excited that for a few moments they had all tried to speak at the same time, ending up laughing. They had all gone out for a celebration dinner and the evening had been magical. There was so much love binding them together. For the first time in months Thembi had not felt the least bit self-conscious about being on crutches in public, nor had she envied Nomalizo in any way. She did feel a small twinge of sadness as she remembered her own engagement dinner, but she pushed the memory aside, determined not to let anything spoil this very special occasion.

Thembi sighed, deciding it was time to go back inside when she felt a prickle of awareness and knew she was no longer alone. It was a sensation she had not experienced since the night of her birthday party.

'*Sawubona*, Thembi,' said the voice behind her.

She whirled around, losing her balance, and he quickly reached out his hands to steady her.

'Mduduzi,' she whispered, her eyes enormous in her face. 'What are you doing here?'

'I've come to take you home, *mayi dali*,' he said, his voice low, not quite steady.

He tried to pull her closer to him and she started to sway towards him when she remembered his arm around the shoulders of the woman as they left the hall on the night of the concert.

'Don't touch me!' she cried, drawing back as if she'd been stung. Immediately his hands dropped to his sides.

'Why not? Why the hell shouldn't I touch you?' he demanded furiously. 'You're mine. You have been ever since the night we met.'

'Oh yes?' she said. 'Well, it didn't take you long to find a replacement for me after we broke up, did it?' she asked, her eyes flashing with temper. Her limbs were trembling so much she had to hold on to the bench to keep from falling.

He stared at her incredulously. 'What are you talking about? I've never so much as looked at another woman since we met, so you'd better explain yourself.'

'Oh Mduduzi, please don't lie to me! I saw you on the night of the concert. I saw you leaving the hall with a woman – a very beautiful woman.' She sighed, her shoulders slumping dejectedly, her anger dying.

Understanding caused his anger to drain away and lifting a hand he gently stroked a finger down her cheek.

'*Sithandwa*, I'd never lie to you. That was my cousin with me that night.'

'Lindi?'

'Yes. Lindi. She had to bring her youngest son to see a specialist and he was admitted to hospital for a couple of days for observation. I took her to the concert with the intention of introducing her to you but by the time the show was over I couldn't face it. I didn't know if you'd even speak to me after the dreadful things I said to you at our last meeting.'

'There's nothing to forgive. I deserved all I got.'

'You sang like an angel that night and I have never seen you look so heart-breakingly beautiful. I ached to take you in my arms and never let you go,' he said.

'Oh Mduduzi, you'll never know how I felt when I saw you with your arm around another woman. It was one of the worst moments of my life,' admitted Thembi, her voice choked, her eyes clouding with remembered pain.

'Dammit, Thembi, we've been hurt enough and wasted too much time already. Come here where you belong,' he said roughly, gathering her urgently into his arms. She went willingly as he pulled her close and bent his head to cover her mouth with his in a kiss of total dedication and adoration as she surrendered herself unconditionally into his keeping.

When he finally released her mouth she collapsed against him, her head resting on the solid wall of his broad chest, her arms clinging about his waist, his holding her close while he rubbed his cheek across the top of her head.

'I love you. You know that. And I know that you love me just as much. What we have, *gugu-lami*, my treasure, is perfect. It always has been and it always will be. Please, don't ever send me away again. I don't think I could take it a second time. Life without you these past months hasn't been worth living and all that kept me sane was the encouragement I got from your parents and the advice I got from Nomalizo.'

'Nomalizo? You asked *Nomalizo* for advice?' she pounced, her voice rising sharply.

'Yes, my *sithandwa*, Nomalizo.' He went on to tell her about their meeting after Thembi had broken their engagement. 'You have no need to be jealous of anyone. You're all I'll ever want.' He kissed her lingeringly, his arms supporting her against him, his one hand on her head, his fingers rhythmically massaging her scalp. Suddenly his arms tightened convulsively about her, crushing her to him so that she could scarcely breathe.

'Dear God, Thembi,' he said, his voice tortured, 'I've missed you so much. I haven't been able to get you out of my mind for a moment, day or night. When your father phoned to tell me you were coming home and it was obvious that something had happened to bring back our old Thembi,

I told him I was coming to fetch you. I flew down this afternoon. I also told him that we wouldn't be leaving here until you'd promised to marry me. Trust me, *gugu-lami*, because in future I don't care what the problem is, we'll solve it together.'

Her mind turned fleetingly to Debbie and with a silent prayer of thankfulness for her own good fortune, she lifted her face and gently kissed Mduduzi's mouth, her fingers splayed on either side of his face as she gazed adoringly at him.

'Mduduzi, my dearest Mduduzi, please hold me close and don't ever let me go again,' she pleaded, her eyes shimmering with love and unshed tears.

'I have no intention of ever letting you go again,' he replied gravely, his arms like steel bands about her body. A few minutes later he helped her to sit on the bench, then taking her ring from the inside pocket of his jacket, he again slid it on to the third finger of her left hand, repeating the words he had spoken once before. 'With this ring I put my heart and life into your keeping. Guard them well, my love.'

'I will, I promise. And this time I really mean it, no matter what happens,' she replied in a choked voice.

They sat for a while, arms about each other, not quite believing that they were once again together, determined never again to be parted.

'Come, I think we'd better go inside,' he said presently. 'By now everyone must be wondering what is happening out here.' He grinned as he stood up, fetched her crutches and helped her back to the house.

'They knew you're here?' she asked, surprised.

'Of course. How do you think I knew where to find you?' he replied, eyes twinkling down at her.

'I didn't think. I *couldn't* think, not once I'd seen and touched you again,' she said, a grin of pure devilment lighting her face and he threw back his head and laughed delightedly.

The excitement and happiness which they took with them when they went indoors, together with Nomalizo and Mandla's, stayed with them throughout their trip home.

As the men took it in turns to drive, they decided not to break the journey for an overnight stop, and it was quite late when they drew up in front of Thembi's home.

They all went inside to greet her parents, who were waiting for them. They were welcomed with congratulations and kisses as well as laughter and a few tears shed by Dikeledi. As Nomalizo was anxious to get home she and Mandla left soon afterwards, promising to call round the next evening.

'We'll all be here,' Thembi said happily, slipping her arm through Mduduzi's.

After they had driven away, Thembi turned to her parents. Mduduzi held her crutches while she hugged each of them in turn, then putting them down, he bent and lifted her into his arms and carried her through to the lounge where he seated her on the sofa, settling himself close beside her.

Dikeledi had coffee and sandwiches ready for them and as they ate Thembi told them about her holiday and then, eager to share her soul-searching experience with her family, she told them about Debbie and John and how she had, through their tragedy, found her own salvation. When she had finished, none of them spoke. They simply gazed at her with sad expressions on their faces. She could see how deeply moved they all were.

'From now on there's to be no more sadness here. That's all behind us now, but I think we've all learned from this to appreciate and treasure what we have. I know I did. And now,' Thembi added, her happiness breaking into her voice, 'we have a wedding to plan!'

———— ♥ ————

Thembi found it difficult to believe that this was her wedding day, that the ceremony which would bind her to Mduduzi was shortly to take place. So much had happened in the last few weeks and yet the time had flown.

She stood in front of the mirror, settling the coronet of flowers firmly on her head, the bridal veil billowing out behind her as she lifted it away from her face.

The heavy, white embossed brocade gown hugged her breasts and waist snugly, the flared skirt falling into deep folds to just above floor level, with the toes of her white boots peeping out as she moved.

She lovingly fingered the gold heart-shaped locket with a small ruby embedded in the centre, which hung from her neck. It was a wedding gift from Mduduzi.

She sat down and studied her reflection in the mirror then smiled as her thoughts wandered back over the last six hectic weeks.

Christmas had come and with it the true spirit of the festive season had filled her home. Mduduzi had closed his office for the week between Christmas and New Year and had spent the whole time with them.

The pile of gifts under the huge tree in the lounge had been opened amid much laughter, surprise and awe as Thembi lifted a delicate necklace of gold filigree from the velvet bed inside the hand-carved wooden jewel box from Mduduzi.

After lunch they had filled both cars with gaily wrapped gifts, then gone to the home of safety where Dikeledi frequently helped, and spent one of the most satisfying afternoons of their lives with the children and staff.

———— ♥ ————

Thembi had had her car converted and was able to get about by herself. She had gone shopping for her trousseau and to the dressmaker for fittings for her wedding dress. She had also visited the convalescent home a couple of times to see Jean and the staff. With every day she had grown more confident and was doing what she had said she wanted to – she was really starting to live again. She was once again independent and with Mduduzi back in her life she had everything she needed to make her happiness complete.

He had spent every evening with her, hurrying eagerly to be with her at the end of each day and staying for dinner each night. On the nights he did not take her out he had been content to sit quietly talking to the family, happy as long as she was near him. It was as if he feared she might suddenly disappear from his life again and she would often look up to find his eyes fixed on her. She had known instinctively what he was feeling and would take his hand in hers and gently squeeze his fingers. The love they shared had grown stronger and deeper with each successive day.

Mduduzi's parents had flown up for the wedding and had been staying with him in his apartment. He had brought them with him to dinner in the evenings and the two families had got to know and like each other during that time. His parents loved Thembi as much as he had once said they would.

———— ♥ ————

Nomalizo and Mandla were to be married in three weeks' time and Mduduzi had promised them that he and Thembi would be back from their honeymoon to be with them.

The traditional *lobola* – the bride-price the groom had to give the bride's parents before a marriage could take place – had been paid and there was nothing standing in the way of the wedding ceremony, after which a reception was to be held at the nearby country club.

Urbanisation had, to a great extent, done away with most of the old Zulu traditions of the time when Thembi's grandparents were young. A wedding those days was a totally different thing to what it was today and she felt a twinge of regret at their passing.

Thembi was brought back to the present by a knock on the door, followed almost immediately by Nomalizo popping her head around it before coming into the room. She came to stand behind Thembi, putting her hands on her shoulders as they looked at each other in the mirror.

'How's my head-dress?' asked Thembi, her hands going up to her head.

'You look beautiful,' replied Nomalizo, helping her to pin the coronet securely in place.

'So do you,' replied Thembi, standing up and turning to her cousin, looking her over with a critical eye. The sleeveless gown of turquoise brocade was cut on the same princess line as was Thembi's, and the long pink lace gloves and the frothy concoction of pink lace and tiny rosebuds on her head completed the picture of beauty she made.

'Thanks for being with me today,' said Thembi softly, bending forward to kiss Nomalizo on the cheek.

'Thank you for asking me to be your bridesmaid,' was the gruff reply. 'Come along, it's time to go. Mduduzi and his parents called for your mother a few minutes ago and your father is getting agitated,' she added with a smile, passing the crutches to Thembi. 'I'll collect our bouquets as we go out. They're on the dining room table. Ready?'

'As I'll ever be. Let's go,' replied Thembi gaily.

When they arrived at the church, Maliyeza and Nomalizo helped her out of the car and Nomalizo carried Thembi's bouquet. As they reached the door leading into the church, Thembi stopped and gave her crutches to her father.

'Leave them at the back, Baba. We can pick them up later. I won't be needing them for a while,' she said, a jubilant smile lighting up her face. 'I've been secretly practising walking without them for weeks. I wanted to surprise everyone – and from the look on your faces I've certainly succeeded very well,' she couldn't resist adding, her eyes twinkling mischievously.

For a moment both Maliyeza and Nomalizo looked stunned, then they beamed delightedly at each other, and then at the bride.

Maliyeza bent and kissed her cheek. 'That's my wonderful girl,' he said proudly.

'Fraud,' whispered Nomalizo, smiling lovingly at her cousin.

She handed Thembi her bouquet and watched as she took her father's arm, holding on firmly as the organ started to play the time-honoured 'Here Comes the Bride' and they started to move towards the altar.

Something in the atmosphere and the sound of faint gasps from the congregation alerted Mduduzi and he turned his head to see the cause. He stared for a moment in blank amazement and then he turned around completely and watched, his eyes ablaze with love and pride, as his beloved Thembi walked slowly, confidently and triumphantly down the aisle towards him and their future.